Bruce paused at the door and wound down the window. Halfway, it stuck. Bruce put pressure on the winding handle, but the window wouldn't budge further.

He stepped down from the cab and took his screwdriver from his kit.

'Don't bother,' said Chapman. 'It's been like that for months.'

'It's no trouble. I'll save [illegible] intenance.'

He climbed bac [illegible] wed the interior panel of [illegible] was peering at Cha [illegible] driver was now consp [illegible]

Bru [illegible] ss, was a soft leather [illegible]

EVAN CHRISTIE

# The Collectors

**GRAFTON BOOKS**
A Division of the Collins Publishing Group

LONDON GLASGOW
TORONTO SYDNEY AUCKLAND

Grafton Books
A Division of the Collins Publishing Group
8 Grafton Street, London W1X 3LA

A Grafton Paperback Original 1986



ISBN 0–586–0–06837–6

Printed and bound in Great Britain by
Collins, Glasgow

Set in Times

# Chapter One

The twenty-eight-foot sloop 'Lotus' rode the gentle waters of the Channel towards Wrelling Harbour. It was a clear morning, and herring gulls drifted languidly over the white-gold beaches along the Dorset coast. Harry Caines, at the helm of the sloop, steered expertly between the sandbanks which flanked the main channel entrance to the harbour.

The 'Lotus' flew a yellow flag which indicated that it had come from a foreign port. Entering the broad sweep of the harbour, Caines tacked past a wooded island, following the deepwater channel towards the town quay. A tall slim man in his early forties, Caines was dressed in a weather-proofed jacket and thick corduroy trousers. His dark hair was swept back from his face by the sea breeze. Picking up a pair of binoculars, he focused on the coastline of what was to be his new District.

Steadying his hands against the gentle swell of the waters, Caines panned the binoculars along the waterfront. Yachts and pleasure cruisers were dotted along the town quay, backdropped by a line of well-kept buildings which offered the traditional amenities of a modern port. There were shipping agents, chandlers, restaurants, coffee shops and quayside pubs. Opposite the quay were the commercial wharves and the roll-on roll-off ferry terminal with its Customs warehouses and offices.

As the 'Lotus' approached the quay, Caines picked out the Custom House, a compact and elegant Georgian building of red brick and white painted stone. Curving stone steps led up to a porticoed entrance from which a white flagpole jutted. The building stood on the quayside, with only the harbour road between it and the water.

Panning to the east, Caines saw the Customs Harbour Launch, 'The Seal'. The helmsman was a bearded man in the dark blue uniform and peaked cap of a Customs officer. He, too, was using binoculars, and Caines followed his line of vision until he picked out an expensive-looking cruiser moored in one of Wrelling's affluent marinas. Breakfast was being served on the cruiser by a steward, and a middle-aged man dressed in white was in earnest conversation with two other men.

Caines swung his binoculars back to 'The Seal'. The officer was still studying the trio with great interest. Then he suddenly rose and went to the radio as if in response to a call. Caines checked the cruiser once more. The meeting between the three men was breaking up, the man in white bidding the other two farewell as they went ashore. And the Customs launch now began to head quickly towards the town quay. Caines lowered his binoculars. Nothing in his face betrayed the curiosity he felt.

'When's our new boss due?' Nigel Markham asked Alyson Bentley.

She shrugged. 'Some time before nine, I expect.'

Nigel glanced at the clock on the Long Room wall. It was 7.45.

'Maybe he'll be on the 8.15 train,' he suggested.

Alyson smiled. 'You eager to meet him, Nigel?'

'A little gesture, I thought. You know. Best foot forward.'

'Enthusiasm is one thing, Nigel.'

'Oh, I wasn't thinking of impressing him or anything.'

'Anyway, he's probably driving here.'

A yachtsman entered and stood at the counter. The Long Room wasn't exactly long – it was simply the name given to the public office in a Custom House, a tradition dating back to the Long Room in the London Custom House built by Sir Christopher Wren in 1671.

'Good morning, sir,' Nigel said brightly as the yachtsman deposited a form on the desk. 'Ah, your 1328. Had a good trip, sir?'

One of the telephones rang, and Alyson picked it up. She was an attractive woman in her early thirties who had joined the Customs four years previously and was now an Executive Officer. Both she and Nigel were in uniform, and her blonde hair was tied up under her navy-blue hat.

The call was from Westholme Airport to the north-east of Wrelling. A flight en route to Heathrow was being diverted there due to weather conditions, and Customs officers would have to be on hand.

Alyson went over to the radio to contact Calvin Sampson on the launch. As a Higher Executive Officer, Calvin was her immediate superior.

'What's up?' Nigel wanted to know.

Alyson waved him quiet and waited for Calvin to respond. When he did so, she explained the situation to him.

'I'll come in immediately,' he told her. 'Give Tom a ring. We're going to need him.'

Alyson returned to the phone and dialled Tom Gibbons's home number.

'You'll have to mind the shop,' she told Nigel.

Nigel, a young Assistant Officer, did not look pleased at the prospect. 'Supposing the new Surveyor arrives?'

'A moment ago you wanted to meet him.'

'Being in charge is different.'

'You'll grow into it.' She heard the phone being picked up at the other end of the line before the voice of a young woman said, 'Hello?'

'It's Alyson Bentley, Mrs Gibbons – Customs. Sorry to disturb you. Is Tom there?'

'Just a minute.'

Sue Gibbons was lying in bed while her husband shaved in the adjoining bathroom. Putting a hand over the mouthpiece of the receiver she said, 'Tom, it's Alyson Bentley.'

Tom Gibbons came into the doorway and made an 'I'm not here' gesture. But Sue held the receiver out to him impatiently. Reluctantly he took it from her.

'Hello, Alyson. What's up?'

He listened, then began to nod, aware that his wife's eyes were on him throughout. 'Yes, yes – I see. If Calvin's on his way in, I'm not needed, am I? You'll have enough people to cope. . . Yes, I realize you're only doing what he asked you. All right, I'll come in.'

He replaced the receiver, not looking at his wife. Dark hair covered his broad chest, and traces of shaving cream still clung to his chin. He was in his late thirties, and had been a Higher Executive Officer at the Custom House for the past four years.

'Well?' Sue said.

'A little emergency.'

He did not elaborate. Sue gave an irritated sigh. 'Oh God, you and your Official Secrets Act.'

Tom stared at her. A breakfast tray sat on her lap, holding a grapefruit, cereal, toast and coffee. She was blonde and beautiful – and only twenty-two. Her hair tumbled about her shoulders in curls, and her face had an elfin look which he had always found irresistible. They had married four years previously.

'As if you'd be interested if I told you about it,' he said. 'Calvin thinks I should go on duty.'

'Now?'

'Now.'

He was already heading back to the bathroom. Sue said, 'Daddy's giving that lunch today, and you're expected.'

'How could I forget?'

'You'd better not, mate. He wouldn't like it. And don't forget that if it wasn't for Daddy, we'd be living in a council house.'

'So you keep reminding me.' Tom stared around the bedroom, which was tastefully furnished in pastel shades of pink and green, with furniture in white. It was pleasant and comfortable – but not comfortable enough for Sue.

Tom entered the bathroom and studied his face in the mirror. He heard Sue say, 'If you're going into town, you could pick up –'

'I'm not going into town.'

'Oh?'

'Westholme. The airport.'

'How exciting for you.'

Nigel was trying to ring Bruce Tomlin, another Executive Officer based at the Custom House. But there was no reply.

'He's not at home,' Nigel said to Alyson.

'I know where to find Bruce,' she replied. 'He'll be at Hayden's Bay, doing his trials.'

'Grasses?'

'Grasses. I'll pick him up on the way.'

She rose from her desk, then paused to peer around the Long Room, with its clutter of papers and used coffee cups. 'Do a bit of tidying up here before the new boss arrives, Nigel.'

And then she departed, heading outside to where her white Jeep was parked.

She drove west, out of the town, past mud flats and heaths and tree plantations. Presently she reached an isolated bay surrounded by low cliffs studded with gorse and broom. She stopped the Jeep and climbed out, peering over tufted dunes.

'Bruce,' she called. 'Bruce! Can you hear me?'

A breeze blew into her face, carrying the smells of the sea. Black-headed gulls were wandering along the waterline, searching for food. But there was no sign of Bruce.

She called his name again, louder and more impatiently. Suddenly she saw him, crouched in a depression near the tide line. He was wearing wellingtons, an olive-drab jacket and a woollen hat. Trowel in hand, he was planting marine grass, and beside him was a large tray holding pots of his various samples.

'Bruce!' she called again, gesturing for him to join her.

Bruce, finally hearing her calls, straightened.

'There's an emergency,' she called to him.

'What?'

'We've got an emergency. At Westholme Airport. Come on, you're needed.'

They were finally in proper hearing distance of one another. Bruce picked up his tray of pots and showed it to her.

'They've got to go in,' he said. 'You don't understand trials, Alyson.'

'This won't wait, Bruce. Come on.'

'It's my rest day.'

Alyson did not bother to argue. She turned and began walking back to the Jeep. Bruce paused, then shrugged before beginning to plod his way through the sand after her.

Alyson climbed into the Jeep and started the engine. Bruce was still some distance away, but now he began to hurry. She opened the passenger door as he approached with his tray.

In his haste to get the tray into the Jeep, Bruce managed to overturn a pot and spill earth over the seat.

'Oops,' he said. 'Sorry, Alyson.'

'Get in.'

'Let me clean it up.'

'There's no creativity without dirt, Bruce.'

He smiled and stabbed a forefinger at her. 'Freud.'

'So you didn't waste all those years at university.'

Bruce pulled the door shut behind him. 'Universit*ies*. I hope not. Do much with Freud in the Wrens, did we?'

She clipped her seat-belt together. 'Give you nightmares

if I told you.'

'Oh?'

'Belt up, will you? A 747's being diverted to Westholme.'

'Ah.' Bruce fumbled with his belt while peering down at his wellingtoned feet. 'Then I'd better change my clothes, hadn't I?'

Alyson's reply was lost in the roar of the Jeep's engine as she drove off at speed.

Peering around the Long Room, Nigel wondered where to begin his task of tidying the place. At twenty-four, he was eager to prove himself as an efficient officer, but this particular task looked daunting. Piles of paperwork littered all three desks, and there were used coffee cups, paper plates and unemptied ashtrays everywhere. Even the potted plants on top of the filing cabinets looked somehow untidy.

A pile of *Portcullises*, the Customs newspaper, lay on the counter, and Nigel decided to start with these. They were covered with a layer of dust, and Nigel made the mistake of blowing on them. A cloud of dust erupted into his face, causing him to cough and splutter. He went over to the window which looked out over the harbour and tried to open it. But the window was stiff, and it took some heaving before it finally opened.

Turning, he saw that a man in a dark blue suit and white shirt and tie had entered and was standing at the counter.

'Ah,' said Nigel, going over to him. 'Good morning, sir. Can I help you?'

The man put an entry form on to the counter. 'My 1328.'

Nigel was thrown for a moment by the idea of a yachtsman in a suit. He picked up the 1328, a declaration of intention for all UK-based yachts which had visited overseas ports.

'Yes,' he said. 'We saw you come in. We'd have got round to you, sir, but things have happened this morning.' He removed the Customs' copy of the form and handed the bottom copy back to the man. 'I assume you gave Customs notice of departure, sir?'

'At Falmouth,' the man told him.

'Yes. And you're from foreign. Nice trip, sir?'

'Yes.'

'And how long have you been away?'

'A fortnight.'

'You're alone?'

'Yes.'

'And you've got nothing other than goods declared?'

'No.'

'Well, that'll be all right then, sir. Thanks for popping in.'

'I'm not going to be boarded?'

'It'll be all right, sir.'

The man reached into his jacket pocket and withdrew a commission.

'Harry Caines,' he said. 'Your new Surveyor.'

Nigel could not hide his surprise.

'Ah,' he managed to say. 'Ah, good morning, sir. I was doing a bit of tidying up.' He tried to indicate where he had been tidying, then decided against it. 'There's a diversion, sir. Heathrow and Gatwick are down with fog. We've got a jumbo coming in to Westholme.'

Caines had suspected something was up. On mooring at the quay, he had gone below to change into his suit. As he was emerging, a woman officer had appeared from the Custom House and driven off in a Jeep. Soon afterwards the bearded officer from the launch had also driven by.

'When is it due?' Caines asked Nigel.

'In about forty minutes, sir.'

'How far is Westholme?'

'You could be there in time, sir.'

'Customs car available?'

Nigel was already plucking the keys from the board.

'If you drive along the quay, sir, then turn left on to the A38. That'll take you straight there.'

'And arrangements have been made for extra staff at the airport?'

Nigel nodded. 'That's why we're a bit light-handed here, sir. That's why there wasn't someone to meet you.'

Caines smiled faintly. 'Who's the HEO on duty?'

'Mr Sampson, sir.'

'He was on the launch earlier?'

This time Nigel hid his surprise. 'That's right, sir.'

'And you are?'

'Nigel Markham, AO, sir.'

'How many passengers on the jumbo?'

'Three-fifty, sir.'

Car keys in hand, Caines made to leave. But he paused in the doorway and turned back.

'Find somewhere less conspicuous for those newspapers, Nigel. After all, this is a Long Room, not a reference library.'

And then he was gone.

Nigel studied the pile of newspapers. He squared them, and was about to carry them over to a desk. But instead he paused and went over to a telephone. He'd better ring the airport and let the others know that the new Surveyor was coming out.

But Caines reappeared in the doorway as he was picking up the receiver. Nigel froze like a schoolboy caught in a petty crime.

'No need to ring the airport, Nigel. After all, everyone should know I'm due in today, yes?'

Caines disappeared again without waiting for a reply.

# *Chapter Two*

Westholme was a modest-sized airport, nestling between farmland and villages several miles north-east of Wrelling. A line of private planes stood at the end of a runway opposite a twin-piston-engined passenger plane. The control tower, hangars and passenger terminals were concentrated at the southern end of the airport.

Tom Gibbons drove his black B registration Jaguar XJL into the compound and pulled up outside the Customs Hall. He wore a smart grey suit over a shirt and tie. Despite sensational newspaper stories about huge drug hauls at airports, Tom knew that such incidents were rare. Most of a Customs officer's time was spent in routine checking of passengers' baggages or goods in cargo warehouses. They seldom seized anything more exciting than a few bottles of whisky or the occasional box of cigars.

The Customs Hall was a small facility, and an extra trestle table was being placed in the green channel when Tom entered. Calvin, Alyson and Bruce were already there – Bruce now in uniform like the others. His greying hair was cropped short, and he looked every inch a Customs officer. He was several years older than Tom and Calvin but was perfectly content with his rank as an Executive Officer; it gave him plenty of freedom to pursue his abiding fascination with marine grasses.

Tom, still peeved at being called out, waited until Calvin spotted him. Calvin came over and said, 'Sorry I had to call you out, Tom.'

'I should think so, too. Surely you could have handled this lot without me?'

'Come on – with the new man arriving, we've got to show

keen.'

'He's coming here?'

'Not as far as I know. But he might.'

Tom shrugged. 'I'm not too interested in giving good impressions. Not any more.' He stared around the hall.

'Come on,' said Calvin. 'There's going to be three hundred and fifty irritated people in our laps very soon.'

'Why can't you deal with them? You're the great charmer.'

Calvin grinned through his beard. 'I thought you'd like the chance to learn the art.'

'I've got this damned lunch today, haven't I?'

'Father-in-law?'

Tom nodded.

'A small price to pay for the Jag and all the accessories, old boy. I'd swap you any day.'

'Like hell you would. You're not the marrying kind.'

Tom and Calvin had formed a firm friendship when Tom had moved to Wrelling six years previously. They had both been bachelors then, and Calvin still was. A bachelor determined to remain that way so that he could continue to play the field. Tom wasn't sure whether he envied him or not.

Calvin was still grinning at him, and he relented in the face of his continual good humour.

'A bit on edge,' he murmured ruefully. 'You understand.'

'Ambition and frustration,' said Calvin. 'The two don't mix, old son.'

Tom smiled. 'Luckily you don't know about either. You and your launch and your harbour.'

'You'd have made a good Surveyor.'

Tom saw that he was being serious for a moment.

'There'll be other chances,' Calvin added. 'Other places.'

'Not with Sue refusing to budge. Life's too good near

Daddy.'

Calvin did not press the subject. He knew that Tom had been bitterly disappointed not to be appointed the new Surveyor on the death of their old boss George Hartley. Calvin himself had no such ambitions: he had inherited a sizeable share of his father's sale of his fishing business, and he had joined Customs more as a means of being able to indulge his passion for sailing than to forge a great career for himself.

'I've told Nigel to ring us when the new Surveyor arrives,' he remarked to Tom.

At that point they heard the jumbo making its approach. Minutes later, it touched down. All the Customs officers began to take up their positions, ready for the influx of passengers.

'Think he'll come out?' Tom asked Calvin.

'Who?'

'The new Surveyor, of course.'

'George wouldn't have bothered to come out.'

'No, bless his heart, he wouldn't. Good man, George. Great shame. What do we know about the new man?'

The question was addressed to everyone in earshot. Alyson said, 'Mr Caines is from Heathrow.'

'Been doing your homework, Alyson?'

'Bruce has.'

Tom turned to him. 'Well, computer?'

'It was just some idle chat I happened to overhear,' Bruce said.

'And?'

Bruce was reluctant to say anything. Trained in sciences – he had a doctorate in biology – he preferred dealing with facts.

'Come on,' Tom urged him, 'you know how much we rely on that retentive brain of yours. Gossip will do.'

'Well,' he said reluctantly, 'when I was on that course in Southampton last year, Harry Caines's name was mentioned. I overheard this snatch of conversation in the cafeteria, about his work at Heathrow. Apparently he's a bright spark and a good organizer.'

'Is that all?'

'There was something about an accident. Something to do with his family. Something tragic.'

'Go on.'

'It's not the sort of thing you ask questions about, is it? But I gather that the accident happened a couple of years ago. That's all I know.'

Tom eyed him. 'Your infallibility deserted you, Bruce?'

'Perhaps it has.' He grinned. 'But I do know the percentage of white wine in French ham chunks.'

The arrival of the passengers was imminent, so Tom and the others manned their stations. This was the category of Customs work known as Preventive duties – essentially the prevention of smuggling by the crews and passengers of aircraft and ships – and uniforms were always worn by officers engaged in such work.

Tom manned the Green channel with Alyson, while Calvin and Bruce prepared to handle arrivals with goods to declare who would go through the Red channel. Preventive staff also patrolled quays, warehouses and marinas, keeping watch for undeclared or prohibited goods and for illicit landings by ships and aircraft. All travellers entering the UK from overseas were required to declare all articles obtained outside the UK if they exceeded the statutory duty-free allowance.

The passengers began to trickle through. Most headed down the Green channel, though some of these were invited to the counters so that their luggage could be inspected, just in case. All baggage was liable to be selected for examination in either channel, and Customs officers needed to be good judges of character with keen powers of detection or intuition which would help them spot a potential smuggler attempting to pass himself off as an innocent passenger. But it was important to be calm, patient, and, above all, polite. Much of their work involved dealing with people under trying circumstances, and every effort was made to keep tempers cool.

One of the airport staff whom Tom knew appeared and approached the counter. Just behind him came a man in a dark suit who looked like just another passenger.

'Message from Custom House, Tom. Your new boss is on the way over. Nigel asked me to send his apologies that he didn't ring sooner. Apparently he was told not to.'

Before Tom could say anything, the man in the dark suit approached the counter. He had obviously overheard the exchange.

'Harry Caines,' he said to Tom. 'Good morning.'

Tom stiffened. 'Good morning,' he replied. 'Tom Gibbons, sir.'

Caines was peering around him. Both channels were now filled with passengers.

'Alarums and excursions,' hc remarked.

'Everything is under control, sir.'

As soon as it was out, Tom realized that he had spoken somewhat defensively. But Caines merely nodded and said, 'Good. I'll float around.'

He headed off towards the entry side where the passengers were gathering. Alyson raised an eyebrow to Tom. And opposite them Calvin and Bruce registered the fact that their new Surveyor had arrived.

For the moment, however, the passengers dominated their attention. Soon both channels had baggage searches underway. Caines lingered in the background, watching his officers work and studying each new arrival. A middle-aged man in a fawn trenchcoat waited patiently while Calvin searched his briefcase. Bruce, glancing over, noticed that the man had the letters YOK tattooed on his left hand. The search produced nothing, and the man was allowed through. He smiled at Caines as he departed.

Caines smiled back. 'Have a pleasant journey, sir.'

Another man in a dark, well-cut suit approached Tom in the Green channel. He was carrying a briefcase which he put down on the counter. Tom was about to let him through, but Caines gave him a nod to indicate that he wanted the briefcase searched. Tom, unused to a Surveyor who did anything more than a loose supervision of their duties, suddenly felt resentful of Caines's interference. But Caines lingered, waiting for him to go through the formalities.

Suppressing his resentment, Tom said to the dark-suited man, 'Is this all your baggage, sir?'

'Yes,' the man replied.

'Did you pack it yourself?'

'Yes.'

'Do you know what's inside?'

'Yes.'

'Everything belongs to you?'

'Yes.'

'Do you have anything to declare to Customs?'

'No.'

'Do you have cigarettes, tobacco, cigars?'

'Two hundred cigarettes and a bottle of scotch.'

'Any wines or spirits?'

'No.'

'Anything you've bought or been given while you've been away?'

'No.'

'Please open your case.'

At this point, Caines drifted off up the line to where Alyson was inspecting the contents of a tall man in a white West African costume. Picking up a package wrapped in brown paper, she said, 'What's in this package, sir?'

'Some local foodstuffs,' the man replied.

'Nigerian?'

He nodded. 'Some gari. This is the trouble it's going to

bring on my head.'

'What trouble?'

'From my brother, if I open this package. But for you I don't have to, no?'

'I'm afraid I must ask you to open it, sir.'

'He think I steal it.'

'Some gari?'

'My brother he loves vegetables.'

'Open it, please.'

'Maybe this foodstuff, this you are referring to – maybe you think it's not foodstuffs.'

'We'll see, sir, won't we? Please open it.'

Caines moved across to Bruce Tomlin's bench. A middle-aged woman who spoke English with a heavy German accent was presenting him with a long list. On the bench in front of Bruce were two large travelling bags.

'This is the entire list of my contents,' she told him.

The list looked thoroughly intimidating, but Bruce made a show of inspecting it.

'Very comprehensive, madam,' he said.

'So you see I am innocent.'

'Of what, madam?'

'Smuggling.' She said it as if it was a swearword.

Bruce gave a small sigh. 'Did you pack these bags yourself?'

'Who else?'

'Yes or no, madam.'

'You think I am irresponsible? How far is London?'

'One hundred and fifty miles.'

The woman shook her head disapprovingly. 'I provide the list to save time and some fog brings me here to this shed. How far did you say?'

Bruce stared at her. 'Do you have anything to declare to Customs?'

She indicated the list. 'Can't you read?'

Caines smiled and turned back to Tom Gibbons. As he

reached Tom's bench, he saw that up to fifty Rolex watches had appeared inside the bottom lining of the man's suitcase.

Caines and Tom exchanged a brief glance, and Tom searched his new Surveyor's expression for any hint of gloating. But there was none.

The passenger was still trying to pretend that nothing was wrong.

'May I see your passport and airline ticket,' Tom said to him.

Reluctantly the man produced them. Tom checked both items before touching the cigarettes and whisky.

'These are within your statutory allowances,' he said, 'and are returned to you.'

The man was now indignant. 'I paid for them, didn't I?'

'Under my powers as an officer of Customs and Excise I am seizing these watches.'

'Yes, I know. Get on with it.'

'These watches are forfeit to the Crown under Customs and Excise Acts on the grounds that they were concealed in a manner intended to deceive an officer. You are not obliged to say anything unless you wish to do so, but what you say may be put into writing and given in evidence.'

The man's resistance had now crumbled. Tom led him off to the interview room. Caines waited a few minutes before joining them.

The passenger was slumped in a chair while Tom, seated at a desk, made a list of the seized goods.

'The offence you have committed,' Tom said to the man, 'can be dealt with by immediate prosecution or I can report it for action at a later date.'

'Immediate prosecution,' the man said glumly. 'At least that will be quicker, won't it?'

Tom remained businesslike: 'I am arresting you and will take you to a police station to be formally charged.'

Caines slipped out of the room as quietly as he had

entered. All the passengers had now departed, and he joined Calvin Sampson and the others in one of the airport offices, where they were drinking tea.

'If only my German were better,' Bruce was saying. 'I think she brought the whole of Bavaria with her. But she was straight.'

Caines addressed Alyson: 'Your Nigerian?'

'Looked a good bet,' she said. 'But it was gari, sir.'

Caines nodded. 'Better to be sure, though.'

He made it sound like a compliment, and Alyson warmed to him a little. 'Not much like Heathrow, sir.'

'Or Prestwick,' Caines replied.

Alyson was surprised. She had served three years at Prestwick Airport before moving to Wrelling. But it was not something she had expected Caines to know.

Calvin said, 'Done your homework on all of us, sir?'

'Yes,' Caines replied.

Tom Gibbons entered and poured himself a cup of tea.

'Is he processed?' Caines asked him of the Rolex passenger.

'Yes, sir.'

Tom's tone was strictly formal, and the others sensed the tension between him and Caines. All, that is, except Bruce, who had been looking thoughtful ever since they had left the Customs Hall.

'What's bothering you?' Alyson asked. 'I can almost hear the wheels turning.'

'YOK,' said Bruce.

'What?'

'The initials YOK. What do they stand for?'

No one had any idea, but everyone's curiosity was aroused. Tom went to a filing cabinet and withdrew the Suspect Index File which contained information on people who were wanted for questioning or were to be detained for a previous offence.

Tom began to flick through the telexes in the file. Caines

watched him, knowing that something was up.

'You spoke to him, sir,' Bruce remarked to Caines.

'Who?'

'The man with YOK tattooed on his hand. I think he smiled at you as he went out, and you wished him a good journey.'

'I didn't notice the tattoo,' Caines admitted.

'John Arthur Benson,' Tom read from the file. 'Forty-two, five feet eleven inches, brown hair, medium build. Tattooed YOK on left hand. Known for large-scale tobacco smuggling. Absconded between Manchester Airport and police station. If intercepted, please etc. etc.'

'Section 138,' Bruce said quietly. 'Customs and Excise Management Act 1979 – sir.'

Caines turned to Alyson. 'Go and check with Immigration – John Arthur Benson.'

Alyson exited quickly. To Calvin, Caines said, 'The tattoo didn't register?'

Calvin looked a little sheepish. 'We get about a hundred telexes a year, sir. You know that.'

'You were talking to him, sir,' Tom said pointedly. He referred again to the telex: 'Detain immediately before he is allowed to proceed or make any communication.'

Caines took the file from him and read through the telex. At this point Alyson reappeared.

'John Arthur Benson, sir, yes.'

'Ring Mr Browning,' Caines told Tom. 'Investigation Division. Tell him what's happened.'

Alyson said, 'The airline's laid on buses, sir.'

'And they've left?'

'Yes.'

'Where to?'

'To link with British Rail, sir.'

'How far?'

'Ten miles.'

'Right,' Caines said, rising. 'You can drive. I don't want

to get lost.'

Already he was hurrying for the door. A surprised Alyson hurried after him.

Sue Gibbons had finally emerged from a long and luxurious soak in the bath. With a white cotton bathrobe wrapped around her, she padded through into the bedroom. Her two young children, James and Nichola, were engaged in a boisterous game with the Filipino maid, Connie. James, a blond two-year-old, was tugging at Connie's long black hair, while Nichola, aged three, was hanging on to the hem of her blue skirt for grim life.

'All right you two,' Sue said, 'no more.'

The children stopped, then began to mutter sounds of protest. But Sue was firm: 'No, that's it. Off to the beach. And Connie, less sand in their hair this time. I won't be back till late this afternoon, so sort out their lunch.'

Connie nodded obediently, and led the children out of the bedroom.

Sue sat down at her dressing table and ran a brush through her hair before reaching for her make-up case.

A press-button telephone stood on the dressing table, and Sue picked up the receiver with her free hand as she applied eyeliner. She punched out a local number.

'Good morning,' said a voice which she recognized as Nigel Markham's. 'Custom House.'

'Oh, hi, Nigel. It's Sue Gibbons. Is my husband there?'

'Morning, Sue. No, I'm afraid he's not here. He's still out at Westholme.'

'Of course. I'd forgotten.'

'Do you want me to take a message?'

'Just ask him not to forget lunch today, will you?'

'I'll remind him.'

There was a pause. Sue applied more eyeliner.

'You still playing tennis?' she asked Nigel. They had been in secondary school together and had developed a light-hearted relationship for over a year before gradually drifting apart. But that was six years ago.

'Still at it,' Nigel told her. 'How's your game?'

'Special. Very special. You wouldn't recognize my back-hand.'

'No?'

'No. Fancy a game?'

'A game?'

'Tennis, Nigel – you remember. Rackets and nets and little white balls. What do you say? I reckon I could beat you now.'

'No chance.'

'Then try me.'

'All right. I'll still thrash you.'

Sue suggested a time, and Nigel immediately agreed to it. Throughout their conversation her expression had not altered: she was concentrating on her make-up.

She hung up, then applied her lipstick. Afterwards she dressed in a cream silk skirt with a matching blouse which she knew accentuated her lithe figure. A pair of pearl tear-drop earrings completed the effect.

Her blue Sierra was parked outside the house. She climbed into it and drove off.

Her parents' house was a large and impressive Georgian building whose bay windows commanded superb views across the bay from the rise on which it stood. It lay in a leafy, affluent part of the town and was surrounded by a green sea of lawns, trees and sculptured flowerbeds. Everything from roses to exotic lilies bloomed in the garden, and there were rock pools with bridges leading to secluded arbours.

Sue turned down a long drive and pulled up outside the house. The front door was open, and she walked through into the drawing room. Her mother was there, arranging freshly cut tulips in a Canton vase.

Helen Langley was an attractive and young-looking

forty-two-year-old with the same blonde hair and shapely figure of her daughter. She was only nineteen when Sue had been born, and her husband, Jack, was almost twenty years her senior. Her blue eyes had a lazy yet provocative look.

'You're early,' she said to Sue. 'Where's Tom?'

'Westholme. He was called out.'

Helen raised an eyebrow. 'He's not going to miss lunch, is he? That, darling girl, would not go down well at all.'

'He'll be here.'

'Your father's made plans, and you know what that means.'

Sue nodded. Helen studied her flower arrangement and seemed satisfied with it.

'It's odd,' she remarked, 'but I think Jack really wants him in the business.'

'That's because Tom is the ideal number two. And Dad knows it.'

The words were said with a hint of weariness, and Helen gave her daughter an appraising glance.

'You sound disenchanted, darling. All well?'

Sue shrugged. 'I don't know. I suppose I'm just a teeny bit bored, perhaps.'

'Would an iced sherry help?'

There was a sparkle in Helen's eyes. Sue gave a slow smile. 'It just might. A bit early, though, isn't it?'

They shared a giggle, more like sisters than mother and daughter.

'Well, well,' Tom Gibbons said as he waited to be connected. 'Who's got egg on his face, then?'

Calvin stroked his beard. 'He doesn't want to get lost, says the man.'

'How very sad.' A voice spoke at the other end of the line, and Tom said, 'Yes, I'll hold.'

'Tom,' said Bruce.

'Mmm?'

'I didn't connect with YOK until it was too late. We can hardly blame the man, can we?'

But a voice was talking in Tom's ear. It was Bill Browning, from the Customs Investigation Division. The Investigation Division was equivalent to the detective branch of the Customs, most of its officers being engaged in collecting information in connection with attempts to defraud the revenue. The division was based in London, though there were also local units throughout the country.

Tom explained that John Arthur Benson had been identified, but not before he had passed through Customs. Bill Browning took the news stoically: most regular smugglers were slippery types. He thought it likely that Benson would elude them once more, despite Caines and Alyson's pursuit.

Tom hung up, then glanced at his watch.

'I might just about make that lunch on time.'

Calvin grinned. 'Smoked salmon sandwiches and tea in bone-china cups, eh, Tom? I don't know why you bother with the likes of us when you could go into business with a rich father-in-law.'

'I didn't marry Sue for her money,' Tom said seriously.

Calvin was still grinning. 'No?'

'For love, Calvin. You know all about that, don't you?'

'Ah, yes. Makes the world go round, old boy. But marriage is a different kettle of fish.'

'One day your time will come.'

'Never. It's much more fun playing the field.'

Bruce was looking thoughtful.

'Think they'll catch him?' he asked. 'Caines and Alyson?'

Tom looked sceptical. 'I'm off to catch some lunch.'

Caines sat in the passenger seat of the Vauxhall Astra while Alyson drove at speed along a winding country road which was fringed by hedgerows. He had almost taken a couple of wrong turnings on his way out to the airport, and he did not want to risk losing Benson simply because he was unfamiliar with the roads.

They drove through gently winding hills, rich farmland spreading out on either side of them. Villages and small towns were dotted everywhere, looking neat and perfectly at home in their rural idyll. Alyson negotiated the roads with great skill while maintaining a good speed. Then ahead of them they saw a line of Friesians emerging from a field on to the road. Alyson braked gently, bringing the Astra to a halt as the cows made stately progress across the road to the field beyond. Several, however, paused on the tarmac as if deliberately intent on delaying their passage.

Alyson made to put the car into reverse.

'We'll wait,' Caines told her.

She nodded. 'Things tend to be a bit more leisurely in this part of the world, sir.'

'Is that good?'

She peered at him from the corner of her eye, wondering if he was probing. He caught her eye and she smiled. 'What is this life, sir – you know. If full of care. No time to stand beneath the boughs . . .'

'And stare as long as sheep and cows. How far's the station?'

'Three miles.'

'Come on, cows.'

As if hearing him, the last stragglers sidled off into the adjoining field, leaving the road clear. Alyson moved off slowly, then accelerated once they were past the gate. Soon the needle had climbed past 50 again.

'You learned to drive in the navy?' Caines asked her.

Alyson was not surprised that Caines knew she had served in the navy before joining Customs. 'Yes, sir,' she said.

'On land or sea?'

She glanced at him again. 'Shall I slow down, sir.'

'No, no. Just idle curiosity.'

Presently they drove through a village whose neat stone buildings hugged both sides of the road. Glancing at a garage which advertised a taxi and car-hire service, Caines glimpsed a man in a fawn trenchcoat standing beside a blue Rover.

'Pull over,' he said to Alyson.

She had already driven past the village, but she responded instantly to the order, braking and turning the car into a grass verge on the side of the road.

'Benson,' said Caines. 'I'm pretty sure I spotted him in that garage. Would the bus driver have stopped there?'

'If he was asked, he might have.'

Alyson reversed slowly down the road until they were in sight of the garage once more. Now the man who was unmistakably Benson was opening the Rover's door.

Caines quickly got out of the Astra and walked towards the garage forecourt, Alyson following him.

'My powers of observation aren't as bad as some people might like to think,' he remarked.

'Never doubted it for a moment, sir,' replied Alyson.

They walked casually towards the forecourt. But Benson had spotted them. Climbing into the car, he immediately started it and revved the engine before shooting out into the road. The car screeched past Caines, only inches away. It sped off, heading north towards London.

'Damn,' said Caines. 'We'll never keep up with that.'

'Come on, sir,' Alyson replied. 'Let's have a go.'

Caines was glancing around for the nearest telephone, but Alyson had already begun to run towards the car. He hesitated, then went after her.

She had left the engine running and was already moving off as Caines reached the passenger door. He clambered in as the Astra picked up speed. Benson's Rover had already vanished around a bend further up the road.

Privately Caines thought they had no chance of catching the smuggler, but he braced himself against the dashboard as Alyson put her foot down. They caught a glimpse of the Rover, perhaps a mile and several bends ahead of them.

'Hold on, sir,' said Alyson as she accelerated into the curve of the road.

The Rover was the more powerful car, and on a motorway it would have left the Astra far behind in a matter of minutes. But these were winding country roads with few straight stretches, and Alyson used the manoeuvrability of the smaller car to gain ground on the Rover. Caines hung on, white-faced but at the same time beginning to thrill to the chase. Alyson was an excellent driver, in constant motion as she changed gears, braked and accelerated.

Relentlessly they gained ground on the Rover. Caines could tell that Benson had begun to panic, for his car was now weaving from side to side as he tried to maintain speed on the bends. They were so close now that Caines could see a dangling clown in the back windscreen. It seemed to be leaping about, mimicking Benson's panic.

Alyson pulled alongside the Rover. Benson was hunched over the wheel, staring frantically ahead. A right-hand curve loomed. Alyson glanced ahead and saw that the road was clear. Putting her foot down, she accelerated across Benson's path.

The smuggler's nerve finally cracked, and he swerved away from her. The Rover mounted a grass verge and went careering into a hawthorn hedge, scattering a cluster of sparrows.

Alyson pulled over a few yards along the road. Benson was already clambering out of the Rover. Before Caines could move, Alyson leapt out of the car and raced after him. She quickly gained on the smuggler, who swung at her as she closed on him. But she slid under the punch and lunged with a foot, kicking his ankles away from him so that he collapsed into a shallow gully beside the road.

Caines hurried over to the two of them. Alyson was standing over Benson, whose trenchcoat was stained with a green slime from the stagnant water in the gully. He was also groaning.

'Are you all right?' Caines asked Alyson.

'Oh, yes, sir.' She looked as if she was about to rub her hands together in triumph. 'He's just my size.'

Caines peered down at Benson.

'She's broken my ankle,' Benson complained.

'I doubt it, sir. Customs and Excise. You are John Arthur Benson?'

'No.'

'You were on the diverted flight to Westholme this morning, sir?'

'No.'

'Then why have we just experienced this hazardous chase?'

'Didn't like the look of you, did I?'

In an attempt at some dignity, Benson had heaved himself up on his elbows. But this only made him look more dishevelled.

'Yes,' said Caines, 'I can believe that. Now I'd like you to come back to the airport with us – quietly. You and I will sit in the rear of the car. Miss Bentley will drive.'

Benson glanced at Alyson as if she was an axe-wielding maniac.

'You keep her away from me,' he said. 'She's vicious.'

# *Chapter Three*

In the Langley driveway stood a Bentley, a Rolls and several other expensive examples of the motor manufacturers' art. As he turned his Jaguar into a parking space, Tom saw Sue taking her sunglasses from her Sierra.

'You're late,' she said as he climbed out of the car.

'A few minutes.'

'The rumblings have started.'

'That's not my problem.'

'It could be.'

'I've told you before – I'm not leaving Customs.'

'Wait till you're asked, can't you? Daddy may make you an offer you can't refuse.'

They walked towards the house.

'So what's going on?' Tom asked.

'Daddy's trying you out against the local money. See if you fit.'

'I don't. And I'm not going to try.'

'No rows, Tom. I'm not in the mood. Come and be civil.'

She led him out through the house on to a spacious lawn. The two dozen or so guests were standing around white wrought-iron tables which held drinks and hors d'oeuvres. Jack Langley, the grizzled patriarch of the family, was in conversation with a middle-aged man in a white safari suit. The Langley business was extensive, embracing building, property, market trading and the leisure centre trade. Tom had heard that during the war Jack Langley had been involved in black market activities, and he had often wondered if his current business ventures were wholly legal.

Helen Langley appeared and glided up to them.

'Ah,' she said, 'there you are, Tom.'

'As I promised,' Sue said pointedly.

Jack had also spotted them. He led the man in the white safari suit over.

'Made it, Tom, did you?' Jack patted Tom's arm. 'Well done. Have you met Charles Thieron?'

Thieron was a well-preserved man in his forties, with a suave manner.

'No,' said Tom. 'How do you do?'

He did not offer his hand, but the Frenchman smiled pleasantly. 'Very well indeed at the moment, thank you, Mr Gibbons.' He spoke English with only a slight French accent.

'Mr Thieron is in property,' Jack said. And to the Frenchman: 'I know that place you've taken over – splendid building. What sort of lease?'

'Oh, short – three years. But I have options.'

'Do I know it, Daddy?' Sue asked.

'If you don't,' said Thieron, 'I hope you soon will. Tom, can I invite you and your wife to dinner next week. Helen and Jack have agreed to come over on Tuesday.'

Tom was not in the mood for pleasantries or social engagements.

'Terribly sorry,' he said, 'we're out on Tuesday.'

'Soon then,' Thieron said, unruffled.

'Oh, please,' said Sue eagerly.

Thieron drifted away. Jack Langley regarded Tom with a hint of disapproval. 'You're not at your most personable, Tom. We might need his help.'

'*We*?'

Jack nodded. 'Both of us. You don't know what I've got in store for you. Does he, Sue?'

'Not a word from me,' she said.

Winking at Tom, Jack then moved away to chat to another one of his guests, Helen following him. Sue and Tom stood alone, Tom wishing he was somewhere else.

'So what's your father supposed to have in store for me?'

he asked.

'Can't tell,' she replied. 'I promised, you see.'

'Don't play games, Sue. You're too old.'

'Not that old, love. At least, not as old as you.'

Now the veneer of banter had been stripped away and Sue's irritation with him was revealed. When she was angry, she never failed to remind him that he was significantly older than she.

Tom watched the Frenchman talking to a glamorous young woman in a Liberty print dress.

'Is Jack involved with Charles Thieron?' he asked.

'I don't think so,' Sue said.

'Are you certain?'

'It's none of my business, is it? Or none of yours. Yet.'

She walked off, leaving him alone.

A table had been laid out on the verandah, and presently everyone sat down for lunch. The conversation was relaxed, convivial, with Thieron a fund of anecdotes and Gallic humour. Tom sat silent, speaking only when spoken to. He felt out of place simply because he had never cared much for so-called sophisticated people. Everyone at the table seemed to him to be playing a role – disguising their real feelings in a haze of trivial chatter.

After the meal, everyone drifted out on to the lawn again. Tom found himself trapped in a conversation with a local councillor while Sue wandered away with Charles Thieron towards the rock pools. Soon they were secluded from the other guests by foliage. They stood on the bridge, staring down at the flowering lilies in the pool.

'Why did you decide to set up home in Wrelling?' Sue asked Thieron.

'It's the difference,' he told her, 'from Marseilles. And Paris. Here I have peace and quiet and the most beautiful view.'

He was looking directly at her. She smiled and said, 'That sounds very practised, Charles.'

'It's the only way to reach perfection.'

'I can see I'll have to sharpen my own conversation if we're to see more of you.'

'Yes, what can we do about that? Will your husband change his mind about dinner?'

'Not Tom.'

'Perhaps your father will be able to work something out.'

They completed their circuit of the rock pools and returned to the lawn. The guests were now leaving, and Thieron, too, made his departure. Soon only the Langleys and Sue and Tom were left.

'I'd better be getting back,' Tom said.

The four of them walked out to the driveway.

'Jag going well?' Jack asked Tom. 'Now, where are we? Today's Monday. How about lunch on Friday? Meet me at the Yacht Club at 12.30. I'd like a little chat.'

'Not much point in that,' Tom said.

'Yes there is, darling,' Sue insisted. She made a point of giving him a kiss. 'Maybe I'll explain later. Are you coming home?'

'No, I'll go straight to the Custom House.'

He got into the Jaguar and drove away.

'Do I tell him?' Sue asked her parents.

'I think she should,' said Helen.

Jack shook his head. 'No, he can hang on till Friday.'

Shortly before lunch Harry Caines arrived back at the Custom House after delivering John Arthur Benson over to the Investigation Division. Through the window of the Long Room, Nigel saw Caines parking the Astra. He immediately felt anxious. When Calvin had got back earlier he had told Nigel that Caines knew he had rung the airport to warn them of his arrival.

Caines climbed the curving stone steps and entered the Custom House. There were office doors to either side of the buff and grey corridor, and on one door was the sign

WATERGUARD, the old name for the preventive service of the Customs. Caines smiled at the anachronism and opened the door to the Long Room.

Nigel was standing at the counter.

Caines said, 'Show me to my office, please, Nigel.'

'Yes, sir.'

Nigel went to the key-board and plucked the office keys from their hook. But he was agitated and he fumbled them, letting them fall to the floor.

'Something bothering you?' Caines asked casually as he picked them up.

'No, sir. Yes, sir.'

'Well?'

'I rang the airport, sir.'

'In what context?'

'Your arrival, sir. Sorry, sir.'

Caines nodded. 'There's one thing you'd better learn as from this moment, Nigel. Chumminess is a thing of the past in this office. And loyalty of that kind has nothing to do with being professional.'

'No, sir.'

'Now, my office.'

Half an hour later, Nigel joined Alyson and the others at a table in The King's Beam pub for lunch. Calvin and Bruce were there, as was John Bryce, a sixty-year-old Excise officer who was retiring soon. The subject of Harry Caines was on everyone's lips, and Nigel was quick to tell the others what had happened when he had unlocked the door to Caines's office.

'He just stood there, staring. For ages. Then he said very quietly, "Oh my God".'

'Meaning what?' asked Calvin.

Nigel wasn't really sure. 'The decor, perhaps?'

'Thank God I'll be out of it all soon,' said John Bryce.

'Is that disillusionment?' Calvin asked him. 'Or are you

tired of Excise?'

'Hate ripples and fuss,' John said. 'Excise has been all right, but retirement's going to be nicer. Besides, I've seen so many bright sparks come and go.'

'Don't be cynical,' Alyson scolded him.

'The bloom of youth gets worn off you,' John replied wryly.

'Rubbish,' said Calvin. 'There's plenty of life left in you. Watch out for him, Alyson. He's still got a bit of wind in his sails.'

John gave Alyson a wink, and she grinned. 'Oh, John, John. If only we'd met years ago.'

'Don't tempt me, woman. I'm old.'

'Matured.'

'Aye. By distilleries and breweries. Nothing much else. It's time for a change.'

'I think change is going to be the order of the day for all of us.'

Nigel spotted Harry Caines entering the pub. He nudged Alyson as Caines approached their table.

'Do you mind if I join you?' he asked.

'What are you drinking, sir?' asked Calvin, a pint of bitter in his own hand.

'Perrier water, please.'

As Calvin moved towards the bar, Caines said to him, 'You were showing great interest in the marina this morning.'

'Sir?'

'On the way in. You were using binoculars. I couldn't help noticing.'

Calvin glanced briefly at the others. 'Long story, sir.'

'I'm a good listener.'

'Shall I get you your drink first, sir?'

'Please.'

While Calvin was at the bar, Caines addressed the others: 'Do I assume that Calvin's interest in the marina is generally shared?'

Bruce shook his head. 'We don't share everything with Calvin, sir.'

To Alyson, Caines said, 'ID have picked up our Mr Benson from the airport. They tell me he complained about an injured leg.'

'And what did you say, sir?' asked Alyson.

'Didn't know what they were talking about, did I? But then I'm in the dark about a lot of things around here.' He stared at each of them in turn, and there was a challenge in his gaze. 'But things will change, I'm certain of that.'

Calvin returned with his Perrier water.

'So,' Caines said to him, 'what were you looking at this morning? I saw three men on a cruiser, one dressed in white.'

Calvin acknowledged Caines's alertness with a smile. 'He's a Frenchman. Name of Charles Thieron. He has a house in Wrelling.'

'What else?'

'He's new to the District. Been in and out of the town for over a year. The cruiser's his.'

'Typical rich visitor?'

'Rich, certainly. But not typical.'

'Come on, Cal,' said Alyson, 'you just don't like the look of him, do you?'

'I don't really know him,' Calvin replied. 'But I don't go much on the cruiser crowd.'

'He wasn't doing any sailing this morning,' Caines said.

'No, sir.'

'Chats on deck with the other two men.'

Calvin nodded, still impressed.

'So what do we have on him?' Caines asked.

'No more than a hint of a smell, sir. Nothing specific, I have to admit.'

'But you think he's worth watching?'

'Yes, sir.'

'All right, we'll go with your instincts on this one. But keep me informed.'

Caines sipped his Perrier. Nigel asked, 'What are you doing about accommodation, sir?'

'I'll be living on the boat for a while.'

'Would you like me to contact some estate agents, sir?'

'Thank you, Nigel, but no. I'll sort something out in due course. But I want to hire a car for a few days.'

'Leave it to me, sir. No family to worry about then?'

There was a moment's awkward silence. To cover Nigel's gaffe, Alyson said quickly, 'Bruce is very much into grasses, sir. One of the university presses is going to publish a book he's written on the subject.'

'Indeed?' said Caines. 'An author, eh?'

'Unless we protect our coastlines,' said Bruce, 'they'll vanish. Very few people realize how much land is eroded each year. And grasses are the proper ecological solution.'

'He could talk for hours about it,' Alyson said. 'What Bruce doesn't know about grasses is hardly worth knowing about. He's also our Bible. A veritable storehouse of arcane Customs facts.'

'I was in the middle of planting some grasses when Alyson picked me up,' Bruce said. 'It was supposed to be my rest day.'

'So that explains the horticulture in the car,' said Caines.

Alyson said, 'Had me down as a gardener, sir?'

'It didn't quite fit,' Caines replied. He finished off his drink and said, 'Is Tom Gibbons on duty this afternoon?'

'Four o'clock, sir,' Bruce told him.

Caines rose from the table. 'I'd better get back to it, then.'

He departed. As soon as he was gone, Calvin said, 'Well?'

'I think he's going to be all right,' Alyson said.

'I hope you'll be saying that in a fortnight's time.'

'Why a fortnight?' asked Bruce.

'He'll have found his feet by then.'

Suddenly Caines reappeared.

'Calvin, you and Tom are on tomorrow?'

'Yes, sir.'

'Good. A little chat with you both.'

Then he departed again.

Alyson looked at Calvin. 'Still offering a fortnight?'

Calvin pondered. 'He certainly likes to move fast. What do you make of him?'

'He's very calm,' she replied, 'but very bruised as well. Sharp and in a hurry. Upwards, ever upwards, I reckon.'

'This place isn't much of a stepping-stone,' Bruce said.

'He's going to make it one.'

'So you chatted in the car, did you?'

'He said very little, and I listened.'

As Tom was parking his Jaguar outside the Custom House, he saw Harry Caines come ashore from his sloop. Tom, still tense after the lunch with his in-laws, nodded briefly as Caines approached.

'Good afternoon,' he said. 'Someone shown you around, sir?'

'I've had a look,' Caines replied as they climbed the Custom House steps. 'The VAT people are a bit crowded in their offices up there.'

'No more than they deserve,' Tom remarked wryly.

But Caines took the throwaway comment seriously: 'Our main revenue collectors?'

Tom shrugged. 'Sooner them than me.'

'The work may appear boring, but it's vital.'

They entered the building. Tom's tenseness had now grown into a vague irritation. Already he knew he was not going to get on with his new Surveyor. But as a routine courtesy – though not without irony – he said, 'If there's anything I can do to help, sir. . .'

'Show me the sample cupboard,' Caines said instantly.

Tom was surprised. 'Now, sir?'

'Please.'

They entered the building and walked down to the far end of the corridor. The sample cupboard was on the left. Tom opened it with his key. It was filled with a selection of plastic containers, bottles, bunches of dried plants, aerosol cans, a small bale of wool and several brightly coloured packets of jelly fruits.

Caines removed a few of the samples and checked the dates of them.

'Some of these samples are a year old.'

'Yes,' Tom said stiffly.

'I assume you've had reports on them from the Government Chemist.'

'One would assume that, yes.'

'Then why hasn't the cupboard been cleared of all this rubbish?'

Tom stared at him, his irritation mounting into an anger which he was only just managing to suppress. 'You might ask that question elsewhere, sir.'

Caines held his gaze. 'Of my predecessor, do you mean? But he's dead, isn't he? I'm asking you.'

'Look, sir, we're only talking about shelf space.'

'And about what it implies. A lax attitude towards the administration of this office.'

'Who are you blaming? George Hartley? He was a very decent man.'

'A quality which does more for chumminess than results. Districts don't function on back-slapping and esteem. Get this sorted out, please.'

Caines walked away, entering his office and leaving Tom fuming.

The office had been tidied for his arrival, but Caines could see it was just a cosmetic job. Piles of paper and official forms had been squared on the desk as though to suggest organization, but each pile contained a jumble of invoices, correspondence and documents. Caines checked the drawers of the desk. They were also crammed with unprocessed paperwork.

He stared at the map of Wrelling District behind his desk, recalling the briefing he had been given a fortnight previously about his new job. 'Compared with Heathrow,' he had been told, 'Wrelling's a bit of a backwater. The District needs a good shake-up, and we'll be relying on you to use your energy, experience and perception to do just that.' Well, he didn't see Wrelling as a backwater; but it *did* need a shake-up, and a shake-up it was going to get.

Caines went down the corridor into the Long Room. It was empty apart from an Executive Officer who was perusing manifests at one of the desks. The EO made to get up, but Caines motioned to him to continue working.

Spotting a boarding case beside a desk, Caines noticed that one of its latches was undone. The cases were used by Preventive staff when they boarded vessels, and they contained duty slip books, a ready reckoner, scrap paper, a date stamp and rummage tools – equipment used when conducting a search.

Caines put the case on the desk and opened it. He discovered a partly used duty receipt book and a completely used one. The receipts were issued for duty paid on goods, and Caines was not pleased to find the books in a half-open case.

Closing both latches, he replaced the case beside the desk. Aware that the EO was watching him warily, he wandered around the office. He spotted a plumbing press, a pliers-like object used for putting the Customs seal on items, which had been left lying near to the public counter. Caines picked it up and took it over to the EO.

'Lock this away, please,' he told the man.

He continued with his examination, registering the old, non-functioning wall-clock with a scribbled sign saying PLEASE DO NOT REMOVE pasted across its face.

Immediately below it was a functioning electric clock. Document wallets bulged from the crammed drawers of filing cabinets, and paperwork stood in piles on any flat surface. He had seen enough.

Caines went next door to the HEO office. Tom Gibbons was seated at his desk when he entered.

'I'd appreciate a chat at five o'clock tomorrow,' he said.

'Calvin's told me, sir,' Tom said evenly.

'Good.'

'Off home now, are we, sir?'

Caines checked his watch. 'Not at four-thirty. Just going to take a bit of a look around the District.'

A District was the title given to a group of Customs and Excise staff in a given geographical area, and it covered all that staff's work in that area. As Surveyor, Caines was head of the District, his rank being equivalent to that of a Senior Executive Officer at the Customs HQ in London. The regional Division, which embraced six local Districts, was based at Southampton and was controlled by Caines's superior, the Collector, and his immediate subordinate, the Assistant Collector.

Wrelling was a town of over 100,000 people, and Caines drove around it slowly, studying its shops, businesses and entertainments facilities. Sailors had used the harbour's expanse of waters for two thousand years, and the town itself had become a thriving port in the fifteenth century. During the 1700s its brigs had carried Dorset men and supplies across the Atlantic to Newfoundland. Today as many as forty commercial ships from all over Europe traded with the port each week, and there was a ferry service to Cherbourg with three sailings a day. The port had also become one of the leading centres for yachting.

Having scrutinized the town, Caines drove out into the countryside, a land of limestone ridges and fertile soil. Small farms lay everywhere, and a local brewery stood in a broad vale, shrouded by oak and silver birch. Most of the country was still intensely rural, and thatched cottages were not uncommon. This was Thomas Hardy country, though the illusion was easily dispelled by the sight of a space-age grain silo or the motorway which cut through the countryside, feeding a steady flow of summertime traffic into the resort towns on the coast.

Presently Caines turned back in the direction of Wrelling. He found himself on a coastal road which looked out over shingle banks and cliffs which were reputedly studded with fossils. As the light began to fade, he re-entered Wrelling. He stopped at a kebab house before driving on and parking his car near the Custom House.

He ate the kebab aboard the 'Lotus', and afterwards drove the Astra over to the ferry terminal. He was in time to see the evening ferry from Cherbourg berthing under a midnight-blue sky. Lines of container trucks were parked in the terminal, many of them Spanish and Italian lorries with cargoes of washing machines and refrigerators. Other regular imports included European cars, fertilizers, timber and steel coil. Outgoing ships carried Purbeck clay mined locally, latex, barley and British Leyland trucks. The Dutch barn – a double open shed where lorries could be weighed and inspected by Customs officers – stood sentinel at the middle of the lorry park.

Returning to the 'Lotus', Caines changed into a smart black mohair suit before driving on to the town's casino. Earlier he had stopped to inspect a local bingo hall for a similar reason: both places were of interest to Excise officers. Broadly speaking, Customs involved the duties and taxes raised on goods imported into the country, while Excise applied to the same duties raised on goods produced in this country. Excise duties were levelled on such establishments as Breweries, Distilleries, Wine Makers, Betting Shops and Racecourses – not to mention the humble bingo hall and the sophisticated casino.

The casino was a modern and well-furnished place, with

a suitable array of well-heeled patrons in expensive suits and glamorous dresses. Caines moved discreetly but purposefully among the card tables and roulette wheels, his eyes taking in everything. Suddenly he spotted the man he now knew as Charles Thieron. The Frenchman was sitting at a roulette wheel, an elegant-looking woman in a black dress draped on his shoulder. Caines watched him for a while, keeping to the shadows. Then he departed, heading home for his humble bunk aboard the 'Lotus'.

# *Chapter Four*

Nigel dragged a large cardboard box into the Long Room. Alyson was at her desk.

'What's to be done with this old stuff from the sample cupboard?' he asked her.

'You can't destroy them in here,' she told him. 'Any nice perfume? If there is, pour it down the ladies loo.'

'It's awful perfume. So what do I do?'

'Ask Tom Gibbons.'

'He's not talking to anyone. I asked him about these, and he just glared at me. There's an awful atmosphere in there.'

Tom and Calvin's desks faced one another in their office, and both were pretending to work. But both were acutely aware that the clock on the wall showed 4.55. Calvin had spent most of the day cruising the harbour in 'The Seal', while Tom had remained in the office, feeling embattled. He was not relishing the prospect of a 'chat' with Harry Caines.

'Ready?' said Calvin, who seemed to Tom to be infuriatingly relaxed.

'He's been nosing around,' Tom said.

'Caines?'

Tom nodded. 'He'll nit-pick.'

'That's reasonable enough.'

'Let's not be too apologetic in there.'

'Maybe we need a little stirring-up.'

'No apologies,' Tom said adamantly.

It was plain to Calvin that Tom was spoiling for a fight.

'Ease off, Tom,' he said. 'Let's hear what he has to say first.'

'I want to know where you stand.'

Calvin essayed a grin. 'Shoulder to shoulder – if right is on our side. Shall we go?'

Calvin rose from his desk, but Tom didn't move.

'Thieron was at that lunch yesterday,' he said.

Calvin was immediately interested. 'Speak to him?'

'A few words.'

'Such as?'

'Pleasantries, that's all. Do you know anything I don't?'

'Not really.'

'Then why the interest in Thieron?'

'Instinct. It's just a feeling I have.'

'He's a big fish, Cal.'

'All the more interesting – if the time comes. The man's bent. See if I'm not right.'

Tom was still delaying their departure for Caines's office.

'Come on,' Calvin urged him. 'And try to calm down, will you? I know how you feel.'

They went down the corridor and knocked on the door.

'Come,' said Caines.

He was seated at his desk, and he greeted them with a formal but not unfriendly smile. 'Please sit down, gentlemen. I won't keep you long. Since we were thrown together yesterday by the diversion, I'd like to sound you out on a certain matter. But first let's get a few preliminaries out of the way.'

Calvin took a seat, but Tom, still on edge, was immediately on the defensive: 'As long as that doesn't imply laying blame, sir. I'd just like you to know that I considered your predecessor, George Hartley, to be a hard-working and excellent Surveyor. Every member of the staff held him in the highest esteem. And I would most strongly object to any inference of poor management on his part or less than excellent work on ours.'

Caines did not respond immediately. Calvin was mortified by Tom's aggression, and he could see Caines's conciliatory manner giving way to a much harder tack.

'Well, well,' Caines said finally in an icy tone, 'let's look at the evidence of this excellent work, shall we? One – a shambles of a sample cupboard. Two – a partly used and a completely used duty receipt book in an unsecured boarding case within easy reach of the public. Three – a plumbing press left in an equally vulnerable place. Four – a Long Room which looks like a cross between an abandoned library and a rubbish bin. Now these facts don't impress me as suggesting a tight operation. Peripherals in their way, perhaps, but oh so illuminating.'

'George Hartley had cancer and didn't know it,' said Tom. 'What would you have done, sir? Shopped him?'

A flicker of anger crossed Caines's face, but he remained outwardly calm. 'I would, and will do, Mr Gibbons, exactly what my commission requires. Is that understood?'

He waited until Tom was forced to say, 'Understood. But I hope you've noted what I've said. And I think the points you've made are excessively petty, sir. You might find similar little deviations in any Custom House in the UK.'

'How would you know that? Your experience of other Districts is almost non-existent.'

Tom was stung by this comment, and Calvin said, 'That's unfair, sir.'

'It's the truth. And it's high time we in this service knew a little more of each other's work and showed a little more flexibility. From now on, I'm not going to allow officers to be totally shut off within their own spheres as if the rest of the work didn't exist.'

Customs work fell into four main disciplines: VAT, Excise, Customs: Preventive and Customs: Landing and Shipping, the last of these covering the import and export of freight through Customs approved places such as ports and airports. Traditionally officers tended to concentrate exclusively on one discipline, with Tom handling the Landing and Shipping work while Calvin cruised the harbour on Preventive duties.

Tom said, 'We had our reorganization in '76, sir.'

'Which doesn't mean that the process has to stop there, does it?'

Caines and Tom were almost glaring at one another.

'Sir,' Calvin said gently in an effort to dispel the tense atmosphere, 'there's time to talk things over – quietly. Things can be put right.'

'Oh, they're going to be,' said Caines. 'I intend reorganizing the District on a team basis. Half a dozen officers in six teams. No, don't panic. It happens elsewhere in the UK. It means that when necessary officers will get involved in other disciplines within the District.'

Tom could not disguise his hostility to the idea. 'You mean that Calvin could be doing paperwork on the roll-on roll-off terminal, sir.'

'If they need help, yes.'

'And the harbour patrols, sir? When he's pen-pushing?'

'Will not be neglected.'

Calvin did not like the idea either. 'Won't work, sir.'

'It's a crazy idea,' Tom added.

Caines was not ruffled. 'Making officers more aware, more efficient? It will work – I'll see that it does.'

Tom said, 'I understand the new broom syndrome, sir.'

'Then understand this: I'm not open to argument on this matter.'

'Then why consult us?'

'Maybe to gauge the difficulty of the task.'

'It won't work,' Tom repeated angrily. He made to leave.

'Mr Gibbons,' said Caines, 'show me your commission.'

Tom stopped at the door and turned back to face him. 'Are you serious, sir?'

'Show me your commission and your identity card, please.'

Tom was not carrying them; he opened the door.

'Mr Gibbons,' said Caines, 'you are required to carry your identity card at all times. Need I say more about the laxness here?'

He regarded both of them in turn. 'Gentlemen, this is going to be a first-rate Customs operation. And to achieve that, I'll require your full and wholehearted support. Nothing less will do. Is that clear?'

Tom exited, pulling the door shut hard behind him.

## *Chapter Five*

'All right my lovelies,' said Calvin as he left the Custom House with Bruce and Nigel, 'let's have a bet on it.'

'Come on, Calvin,' said Bruce. 'Just because Caines transfers you to a desk job.'

'Not for long he won't.'

'You sound confident. Know something we don't?'

Calvin grinned through his beard. 'Our Mr Caines has been summoned. To see the Assistant Collector.'

'I know that.'

'So things will revert.'

'That's just your frustrations talking.'

Calvin shook his head. 'Caines is moving too quickly, old son.'

'By putting you at a desk?'

'Certainly. It's stupid.'

'You're still in shock.'

'I can cope with paperwork. And his new broom.'

'I wonder.'

'Money where your mouth is, then.'

'So what's the bet?'

'That I'm off that desk in forty-eight hours.'

It was morning, and they were walking along the quayside road towards the roll-on roll-off ferry terminal. Bruce and Nigel were in uniform, while Calvin wore a suit, shirt and tie which looked incongruous on him. They passed 'The Seal', which was moored in the water nearby.

Nigel said, 'Who's going to look after your baby, Calvin?'

'Listen, old son, Caines is going to be read the Riot Act this morning. So in a matter of hours "The Seal" will be mine again.'

'Boarding all that talent from France?'

Calvin grinned. 'A fine relaxation, and why not?'

As they arrived at the terminal, the Cherbourg ferry was in the final stages of docking. They crossed the spacious lorry park, then paused. Bruce and Nigel would go on to the Dutch barn through which the incoming lorries would pass, while Calvin was taking charge of the Entry Processing Unit – the administrative offices which stood near the gatehouse.

'Go on then,' said Bruce, 'get stuck into those forms.'

Calvin looked almost wistful. 'It's against nature, old son – forms and such like.'

'The New Order, Calvin. That's the way it's going to be from now on.'

Calvin pointed to the ferry. '*That's* Customs work.'

'The old Waterguard's dead, Calvin.'

'Good old days, they were. Grab your smugglers, then home for tea.'

'Want to borrow a pen?'

'Your turn will come, Bruce.'

'So you've changed your mind, have you? About Caines?'

Calvin shrugged. 'He won't give in without a fight, will he?'

'Bet's off then?'

'Just get about your work, you two.'

Calvin trudged off towards the offices. Nigel and Bruce headed for the Dutch barn. The Customs office inside the barn held a long counter on which incoming drivers deposited passports and documents giving details of the loads they were carrying. Lorries were examined at random to ensure that the declared load was exactly what was being carried. A metal walkway extending under the ceiling of one shed enabled the lorries to be checked from above where necessary.

Bruce and Nigel were quickly to work as the first of the lorries rolled off the ferry. Once they had passed through the barn, the lorries parked inside the compound until their paperwork had been processed in the EPU and they were given clearance to enter the country.

Usually the work was routine, but there were always unexpected incidents. Nigel and Bruce were dealing with two drivers when there was a heavy metallic crash from outside.

Bruce was quickly on the scene. A large Spanish lorry had bumped into an equally large French lorry. There was no visible damage, but both drivers had emerged from their cabins and squared up to one another. A barrage of bilingual abuse followed with plenty of gesticulations until Bruce stepped between the two men. In effortless French and Spanish he addressed both drivers, quickly pacifying them. Nigel looked on, thoroughly impressed by his colleague's linguistic skills.

Calvin, meanwhile, was huddled over a pile of manifests – lists of freight being carried. He stared morosely at the documents, then gazed out the window. Adrift in a sea of paperwork, he thought, barely registering the red articulated lorry which turned into the terminal from the town.

The lorry's driver, Dave Chapman, was a fair-headed man in his mid-twenties. He parked the lorry without fuss, then climbed down from the cabin before heading on foot back towards the town. He wore faded jeans and a somewhat battered brown leather jacket over a check shirt. Reaching the shopping district, he paused outside a hairdressers with a smoked glass window. The red neon sign above said, KALMAN'S.

Inside, Joseph Kalman, the owner, was making his morning round of the salon. He was a swarthy man in his late thirties, dressed in an open-necked white shirt which revealed an expensive gold medallion on his thickly haired chest. The salon was elegantly furnished in stucco and wickerwork, with potted plants adorning shelves, pedestal ashtrays, and green leather armchairs for the convenience of the waiting patrons. Kalman's assistants were all attractive young women, and his salon was currently the most fashionable in Wrelling.

The twelve work areas all held customers, and Kalman moved from one chair to another, greeting his patrons. In the furthermost work area a good-looking woman in her mid-thirties was having the finishing touches applied to her hair by a blonde assistant.

Kalman took the scissors from her and said, 'I'll finish Mrs Porter, Jan. You attend to Number Three. Make sure her blue rinse hasn't turned green.'

The assistant departed without a word, leaving them alone. Kalman and Mrs Porter exchanged smiles in the mirror.

'How are you, Carol?' he asked.

'Fine. Just fine. Your prices have gone up again.'

'It's inflation, my dear.'

'Have you brought the necessary?'

'Of course.'

Reaching into his pocket, he produced four gold coins in transparent plastic sachets. Carol Porter's hand had already appeared from under the white gown which she wore, and Kalman dropped the coins into it. The hand vanished under the gown as she smiled.

Just then Kalman saw Dave Chapman enter the salon. A flicker of irritation crossed his face. He immediately summoned Jan once more.

'Sorry, Carol,' he said. 'I'll be a couple of minutes. Jan will look after you until then. Get Mrs Porter another coffee, will you, Jan?'

Kalman intercepted Chapman and led him to a doorway at the rear of the salon. They climbed a flight of stairs to the spacious flat above. It was a bedroom-cum-office, lavishly decorated. The bedsheets were purple satin, the carpet a smoky pink, the furniture a brash combination of the antique and ultra-modern. Chapman, in his battered jacket and faded jeans, looked hopelessly out of place.

'What's brought this on?' Kalman said angrily. 'I thought we agreed that you were never to come here.'

Chapman shrugged. 'I just think we're pushing it a bit, that's all.'

'That's all? I have a shop full of customers, but I've got to make time for you to have the jitters. Great. Just great.'

'They're tightening up down there.'

'Where? Who's tightening up?'

'The Customs lot. The faces keep changing. They're asking more questions.'

'Is that a fact? So what do you want me to do? Write out the answers for you beforehand?'

'I'm only saying let's leave off for a while.'

Kalman stared at him before slumping on a tubular leather couch which stood beside a Regency occasional table. He did not invite Chapman to sit down.

'Listen,' he said, 'you're in a business and you work for me. We've built a clientele who rely on us to supply them with cut-rate Krugerrands, and we're not going to stop now. I provide the capital and you provide the conveyance. All you have to worry about is getting the merchandise safely to me. If you're having pangs of conscience, think of it as simply bypassing the VAT on the items.'

'I'm not having pangs of conscience, but it's still smuggling. And I'm worried about making that crossing too often and coming back empty too often. Soon they're going to be on to me.'

Kalman was in no mood for an argument. He shrugged. 'OK, if that's how you feel, I'll find somebody else. Let's have the money back.'

'I didn't say I wouldn't do it.'

'So what are you telling me?'

'I'll do it. But –'

'Then do it and stop bellyaching. Otherwise you're never going to be able to buy that truck you want, are you?'

The office door opened, and Tom looked up from his paperwork. It was Harry Caines.

'I'll be out of the office all morning, Tom.'

Tom nodded. 'Need a guide, sir?'

Caines sensed the sarcasm in his tone.

'A guide?' he said with only a hint of irritation.

'Wherever you're going, sir. I've been in the District a long time. Know my way around.'

'I don't think I'll lose my way, Tom.'

Caines was already heading for the door. Tom said, 'But should we need to get in touch with you, sir?'

Caines turned back to him and smiled. 'I'll be in Southampton. At the Assistant Collector's office.'

'A summons, sir?'

'A meeting, Tom.'

Caines drove east towards Southampton, and an hour later he pulled up outside the modern office block which were the headquarters of the local Division. As he rode up in the elevator to Charles Christie's office he studied his appearance in the mirror and was satisfied that he looked suitably kempt. He had known Charles for many years, but the Assistant Collector was, after all, his immediate superior.

Christie was a balding, thickset man who greeted him warmly on his arrival. A Clerical Assistant fetched them tea in china cups, and when they were alone, Christie said, 'Well, then, I hear you're causing a bit of turmoil in your District.'

'Turmoil?' said Caines.

'This team idea.'

Caines adopted a surprised expression. 'You see flexibility of operation as undesirable?'

Christie smiled. 'I'm listening.'

'It's a simple notion. Give as many people as much experience as possible.'

'But Customs is Customs and Excise is Excise – surely?'

'My District.'

'Agreed. But are you moving too quickly, I wonder?'

Caines eyed him. 'Have you heard something?'

Christie picked up his cup and sipped at it. 'You know how good the grapevine is.'

'And now rumours start.'

'Then reassure me.'

Caines put his own cup and saucer down on the floor. 'Basically, I see the operation as a team effort. I want each member of my staff to get involved in different aspects of the work.'

Christie said nothing to this.

'You don't look convinced,' Caines remarked.

'I'm only suggesting a little more caution.'

'I was told to pull the operation together. Am I to understand that my hands are now being tied?'

'Oh, come on, Harry. We've known one another too long to start sniping at one another.'

Caines was not mollified. 'So then I'm only here to have my nuisance value defined?'

Christie sipped more tea. 'I know what you're about, Harry. I'm well aware of your calibre and I also know you've got problems in Wrelling. But I don't think your team idea will work.'

'Why not?'

'Do you really believe that putting an officer who's spent years in Customs on to something like VAT will work?'

'Where that officer has had relevant experience, yes. Or is willing to train.'

Christie peered at him. 'You know there may be trouble from the Union.'

'How do you know that?' Caines asked sharply.

'Rumblings on the grapevine. And if you go too far too

fast, the Collector will stop you.'

'He was the one who told me to shake things up. You were there at the time.'

'Shake things up, yes. But not tear them apart.'

'I've no intention of tearing them apart.'

Christie paused, then let out a small sigh.

'Look, Harry,' he began again, 'I know how bloody rough it's been for you –'

Caines made a dismissive gesture. 'It hasn't influenced my judgement here, Charles – I'm not on some daft crusade. But I need to know about this grapevine.'

Christie did not prevaricate. 'I chatted to Bruce Tomlin after the last Whitley meeting.'

Whitley meetings were regular negotiations between staff and trade union members, named after their founder, Lord Whitley.

'And someone's been on the phone to you?' Caines guessed.

'The odd word, perhaps,' Christie admitted. 'Relax, Harry. It was nothing improper.'

'That's a matter of opinion. I like arguments up front.'

Christie was silent for a moment, as though weighing up what had been said so far.

'All right, Harry,' he said at last, 'I'll support your idea in theory until I have a chance to evaluate it in practice. But I won't have the District rocked too much. Keep in close touch with me.'

The meeting was over. Caines rose and prepared to leave. As he opened the door, Christie added, 'And get off that boat, Harry. I don't want my Surveyor bobbing about on the water for too long. Bad for the image. Point taken?'

Two faces appeared at the open window while Calvin was gazing impotently at the pile of manifests on his desk. Studiously he ignored them until one of the two coughed.

'Lunch?' said Nigel.

'Go away,' Calvin replied without looking up.

'Hate to see you so unhappy,' said Bruce.

'I'm coping very well, thank you.'

He pretended to study a manifest while Bruce and Nigel waited, keeping their faces straight. Half a minute passed.

'All right,' Calvin relented. 'Bruce – tell me about Mandarins.'

'Ah,' said Bruce. 'Mandarins. An elitist social group, Northern China. Mandarin, the only written language –'

'Fruit, mate, as you know full well. Spanish. Tinned. Imported.'

'Oh. Why didn't you say so?'

Calvin thrust the manifest through the window into Bruce's face. Bruce took it from him and began to study it.

'Paperwork,' Calvin said to Nigel with disgust.

Behind them, container trucks from the ferry were lined up in the lorry park. And Dave Chapman was driving his lorry towards the queue waiting to board the ferry.

'Who was that?' Tom asked Sue.

He had arrived home for lunch as she was putting down the telephone.

'Just confirming a tennis date for this evening,' she told him. 'Thought any more about tomorrow night?'

'Tomorrow night?'

'The casino. We've been invited to the casino.'

Tom shook his head. 'Can't manage it, love. I've got an early start the next day. Sorry.'

Sue sighed. 'Yes, so am I. Everything I plan seems wrong.'

The note of petulance in her voice made Tom bristle. 'I don't like gambling, so I'm not going.'

She stared hard at him. 'And the fact that I do, doesn't matter a damn to you, does it?'

'I came home for lunch, not rows.'

Sue walked over to the window and peered out. She was

wearing tight-fitting designer jeans and a Breton T-shirt.

'OK,' she said, 'so you're not doing Wednesday. Just don't forget about Friday.'

'Friday?'

'Lunch with my father. If you leave him in the lurch, there'll be trouble.'

'I won't forget. Where are the kids?'

'Connie's taken them for their swimming lessons.' She turned to face him again, framed by the sunlit window. 'It's a pity their father can't spare the time to teach them. But he's too busy pursuing his rather unsuccessful career with Customs and Excise.'

Arriving back at the Long Room after lunch, Bruce and Nigel found Alyson on duty.

'You look tired,' Bruce remarked to her.

'That's how I feel. I had another bad night with Thomas. I don't know why he does it. Everything was going so well, and then he starts behaving like a pig again. Look at that.'

She showed them the back of her neck. There was a purple bruise on it.

'My God,' said Bruce, 'I didn't know he was that violent.'

Nigel was horrified at the thought that Alyson had a boyfriend who beat her up. 'Get rid of him, Aly. Nothing's worth that.'

'Can't,' she said. 'Sometimes he's so marvellous – you just wouldn't know. Anyway, it's my problem, and I'll have to sort it out.'

The telephone rang, and Nigel picked it up. After listening, he said, 'Yes, sir, he's just come back. . . Right, sir, I will.'

Nigel put the phone down and addressed Bruce: 'It's Mr Caines. He wants to see you in his office immediately.'

Bruce went down the corridor and knocked on the Surveyor's door.

'Come in,' he heard Caines say sharply.

Caines was seated at his desk, and his expression was stern. Without preamble, he said, 'I've heard rumours about potential trouble with the Union.'

Bruce frowned.

'You're active in it, aren't you? I thought you might be able to tell me what's going on.'

'As far as I know, nothing, sir.'

'Not the impression I got from the AC.'

'Sir?'

'He says he had a telephone call from one of my officers.'

'Oh, yes, sir?'

'And a conversation you had with him after the last Whitley meeting.'

'Are you against Union activity, sir?'

'No, I'm not anti-Union at all, Bruce. But I do object to talking behind my back. Now, about this telephone conversation.'

'That was unofficial, sir.'

'Official, unofficial – what's the difference?'

'There is a difference, sir.'

'That conversation was tantamount to taking an unresolved Union matter out of this District.'

Bruce was not going to be steamrollered. 'I don't see it that way, sir.'

'Then explain to me why objections to my ideas are being reduced to gossip and innuendo.'

'I don't think that's fair, sir.'

'No, it isn't. And it's got to stop.'

The evening sun shone over a line of Lombardy poplars, and Nigel sat on the verandah of the tennis club, gazing out over the green courts. He wore a white tennis shirt and shorts, and he held a racket in his hands. Other players were knocking balls around on one of the courts, but Nigel wasn't registering them. He was thinking of Sue Gibbons and wondering why she had invited him to play tennis after several years in which they had seen practically nothing of one another. He didn't pretend to understand women, but he had to admit that he had been thoroughly pleased to accept.

At this point Sue herself appeared. She, too, was dressed in whites.

'Sorry, Nigel,' she said, pecking him on the cheek. 'Forgiven, am I?'

Nigel caught a whiff of the expensive perfume she wore. Her tanned skin was vividly emphasized by the pure white of her skirt and blouse.

'For what?' he asked.

'Being late.'

Nigel had not even noticed.

'You always were,' he said. 'Late for lessons, late for practice. Late for everything.'

She smiled. 'But I always caught up, didn't I?'

'Come on. I'll take you in straight sets – just like in the old days.'

'We'll see,' she replied.

She took his arm as they headed towards the courts. 'It's good to be doing this again, Nigel.'

'Yes,' said Nigel, thinking that it was, in fact, marvellous.

# *Chapter Six*

'These early shifts,' Tom Gibbons remarked, stifling a yawn.

Bruce Tomlin nodded, staring out through the window of the Custom office in the Dutch barn. Apart from VAT staff, who worked normal office hours, Customs and Excise officers worked shifts and overtime where necessary, weekends and night duty included. Sometimes it played hell with your body clock.

The early morning ferry had already docked, and the first lorries were beginning to emerge. At a desk behind Tom and Bruce, a Special Branch officer was checking through a list.

Suddenly the door to the office opened and in walked Harry Caines.

'Morning, sir,' said a surprised Tom.

'Good morning,' Caines replied.

'What can we do for you, sir?' Tom asked.

'Just feeling my way.'

'Up early, sir,' Bruce remarked.

'Yes. The morning tide woke me.'

'Ah. You'll have to get off that boat, sir.'

'Indeed I will, Bruce.'

Caines walked behind the counter and took up a position where he could observe his officers; both Tom and Bruce were in uniform. Presently the first drivers began to filter into the office with their passports and papers. The second to appear was Dave Chapman.

'Coming back empty?' Tom asked him.

'Yeah. You know what the competition's like. Can't always pick up a load.'

'And you couldn't wait?'

'Had to get back. Family reasons.'

'I see. Any cigarettes, wines, spirits?'

'No.'

'All right then. Thank you.'

Chapman moved away from the counter, and another driver took his place.

Tom and Bruce were kept busy for well over an hour, and all the time Tom was aware of Caines hovering in the background, watching everything. It made him feel nervous and resentful. But he said nothing, concentrating on processing each driver as quickly and efficiently as possible. Afterwards he, Bruce and Caines headed across the lorry park to the EPU. Truck drivers were emerging from agents' offices and heading off to Wrelling town for breakfast or a few hours' sleep.

To Caines Tom said, 'Is Calvin going to be allowed on his launch again, sir?'

'Oh, yes,' Caines replied. 'Do any sailing yourself, Tom?'

'No, sir.'

'Is he very unsettled? Calvin?'

'He'll cope, sir. But it's not really his forte.'

'What about this Frenchman? Is Calvin on to something?'

'He's got a good nose. Useful to have ferreting around.'

'So he shouldn't be wasted on paperwork?'

'Far be it for me to say what's right or wrong, sir.'

Caines peered at him. 'Form-filling adds a little perspective. Obsessions can be dangerous. They can get your feet wet.'

'Calvin's a good sailor, sir. He knows how to keep himself afloat.'

Joseph Kalman stood waiting on a flyover which crossed the motorway a few miles outside Wrelling. His red Alfa

Romeo convertible was parked nearby. Kalman checked his watch and stared down at the sparse traffic on the motorway. Filaments of mist still hung amongst a stand of pines beside the road, but it promised to be a warm, clear day.

Kalman waited patiently until he spotted the red lorry which he quickly identified as Chapman's truck. Then he got into his car and drove down the approach road to the motorway.

The lorry was perhaps half a mile ahead of him, but he gained ground on it easily and pulled alongside it. There was no other traffic in the immediate vicinity. He knew that Chapman had already picked him up in his rear-view mirror, and now the truck driver reached an arm out of the open cabin window and tossed a soft leather pouch on to the passenger seat of the Alfa Romeo. Kalman immediately accelerated away.

'Morning,' Nigel Markham said to Alyson as she entered the Long Room.

She gave a grunt in reply.

'Now what have I said?' Nigel asked.

Alyson merely shook her head.

'Thomas?' Nigel guessed. 'Another rough night?'

She nodded. 'And Chris is coming down tomorrow night.'

'Chris?'

'You don't know about Chris?'

Nigel shook his head. Did Alyson have two regular boyfriends?

'Good,' she said. 'I've still got secrets.'

'You're not telling?'

'No.' She took a pocket mirror from a desk drawer and peered at herself in it. 'I'll have to do something about my hair, won't I?'

'Who for? Thomas or Chris?'

She grinned. 'Why not both of them?'

Nigel did not know what to say to this. But then the telephone beside him rang. It turned out to be a call for Harry Caines from one of the local estate agents. Caines was not yet in – Surveyors worked flexible hours – so Nigel took a message.

When Caines appeared half an hour later, Nigel went straight to his office.

'Excuse me, sir,' he said. 'The estate agents you contacted rang. There's a furnished flat available just around the corner, and someone could show you around it this evening.'

Caines nodded. 'Thank you, Nigel.'

But Nigel lingered uncertainly.

'Was there something else?'

'No, sir. But those flats – well, it's none of my business, but they're holiday lets.'

'Really? Well, thank you for letting me know.'

'Sure you won't change your mind?' Sue asked Tom.

'I told you – I have to be up at five tomorrow.'

'Go on, be a devil for once.'

'You enjoy that sort of thing. I don't. So why mess up an evening?'

She sighed. 'Why indeed?'

Tom watched her put the final touches to her make-up in the dressing-table mirror. He was lying on the bed, the evening paper draped on his lap. Sue wore a black satin dress and the diamond necklace which her father had bought her for her twenty-first birthday. She looked very glamorous.

'Who else is going?' he asked.

'Jack and Helen.'

Tom smiled and shook his head slowly.

She caught the expression in the mirror. 'Now what?'

'Being so familiar with your parents, that's all.'

'It's the generation gap, darling. I do believe you're turning into an old fogey.'

Tom did not respond to the barb. 'Anyone else in the party?'

'Questions, questions. You are a tedious old thing, Tom. Do you really care?'

'Of course I do.'

'Then prove it. Join us.'

Tom shook his head again. 'Sorry.'

The estate agent was young and keen – and nervous. He led Caines around the shabbily furnished flat, doing his best to point out the virtues of the place. There weren't many.

Caines remained silent during the tour, and the estate agent grew more nervous each passing second. He led Caines into the bathroom, and then down the stairs to the kitchen, his voice beginning to falter as he ran out of positive things to say about the flat. There were paintings on the walls, but they did not disguise the drab wallpaper. The furniture was cheap and old-fashioned, looking like something that had been bought from a catalogue twenty years before. The mock-persian carpet was threadbare.

'Of course, sir, we do have flats in the upper range on the other side of town. If you balance the advantages of convenience to work – as this flat certainly has – with perhaps a better neighbourhood. . .'

His voice faltered again. Caines had gone over to the living room window and was peering out. Night was falling, but he could see right out over the harbour. The Custom House was close by.

'This will do,' he said simply.

As the roulette wheel spun, Charles Thieron regarded it impassively. On his right stood Jack and Helen Langley, while to his left was Sue Gibbons. Her hand was resting gently on Thieron's dinner-jacketed arm.

She glanced at her mother, who was looking back at her. A knowing yet admonitory smile formed on Helen Langley's lips, and Sue made to withdraw her hand. But Thieron put his own over hers.

'No, Sue,' he said. 'You're my good luck. Don't go away.'

She smiled, nodded.

'You see?' said Thieron as his number came up.

The croupier shovelled a pile of chips towards him. Thieron then excused himself briefly and entered the men's room. As he stood in front of one of the bowls, washing his hands, a dark-haired man came up beside him. It was Joseph Kalman. He had been watching Thieron at the roulette wheel, and waiting his moment. Now he peered at Thieron in the mirror until the Frenchman looked up.

'Table running for you?' he said.

Thieron did not respond.

Kalman indicated the gold bracelet and gold watch which Thieron was putting back on his wrists.

'You like gold?' It was half a question, half a statement.

'Yes,' Thieron said. 'I like gold.'

'Well, I'm selling.'

'In a washroom?'

Kalman shrugged.

'OK,' said Thieron. 'Show me.'

Smiling, Kalman reached into the inside pocket of his suit and produced a handful of Krugerrands, still in their plastic casing.

'How much?' Thieron asked.

'Ten per cent below.'

'I'll have three at eleven per cent under. It's fortunate that my credit is good here.'

They exchanged the Krugerrands in the washroom, then went outside to the cashier's grille. Kalman watched as a thousand pounds in fifty-pound notes was counted out. Thieron handed the money over to him.

'Thank you,' Kalman said.

'Thank *you*, monsieur,' Thieron replied.

The Frenchman walked back to the roulette table. Sue Gibbons had noticed the exchange of money, but she said nothing. This time she rested her arm on Thieron's shoulder as he made his bet, aware that her mother was still watching her.

The wheel began spinning, the ball hopping and skipping around it. Sue found herself almost hypnotized by the movement. Then the ball began to lose its momentum before tumbling to its final resting place.

Thieron had won again.

'My good luck charm,' he said to Sue as the croupier shovelled more chips towards him. '*Merci beaucoup*.' He pecked her on the cheek.

Sue gave a light-hearted frown. 'That was a little disappointing. What do you think, Helen?'

'Positively chaste,' Helen was forced to agree.

'This is more like it,' Sue said, and she kissed Thieron full on the lips.

'Ah,' he responded. 'Now I see. My apologies. Perhaps you will accept this in return for the luck and the kiss.'

He produced a Krugerrand from his pocket and handed it to her.

'Beware of Frenchman bearing gifts,' said Helen.

'Are you trying to blackmail me, Charles?' asked Sue.

'Now you are both making fun of me,' said Thieron. 'Jack, I need your support.'

Jack Langley had been more intent on the next round of betting. He gave a resigned shrug. 'Nothing I can do about either of them, old boy. Gave up years ago.'

'You mean you allow them to run wild?'

'It's the only way.'

Sue and Helen had moved out of earshot of the men.

'What did Charles give you?' Helen asked.

'Oh, I don't know. A pretty little penny.'

She showed her mother the Krugerrand.

'A pretty little penny indeed,' said Helen. 'It's worth between three and four hundred pounds. What a lucky girl you are.'

Sue was clearly delighted. Thieron returned to her side.

'What happened to Tom this evening?' he asked.

'Oh, he wouldn't budge. Work or something.'

To Jack, Thieron said, 'He's a most inattentive son-in-law.'

'Very true, old boy,' Jack replied. 'But I'm working on him.'

'Tom's not an easy man to persuade,' Helen remarked.

Thieron put his arms around mother and daughter. 'Between the two of you I would think that any man would be – what is the word? – putty?'

Mother and daughter smiled the same smile.

'Yes,' Alyson was saying into the telephone, 'I'm on duty tonight. It's part of Caines's new flexibility. As many of us as possible, doing as many different jobs as possible. I'm in a sort of team now, with two HEOs, two EOs and AOs. . . No, I'll be off tomorrow afternoon, so I'll see you then. . . Drive carefully, Chris. . . Yes, I love you, too. Good-night.'

She put the receiver down just as Harry Caines appeared in the doorway of the Long Room.

'Everything all right?' Caines asked.

'A few yachts in from foreign, sir.'

'Coping?'

'For an Excise lady thrust into Customs, not too badly, sir.'

'Good.'

Caines turned to leave. Alyson said, 'Sir?'

'Yes?'

'Chris – uh, Chris Lucas – was just on the phone. He sends his regards. I didn't know you knew one another.'

Caines nodded. 'I didn't know you'd worked with Chris. There's no mention in your file of you ever being involved in the Investigation Division.'

'It was in an unofficial capacity, sir.' Several years previously Alyson had been employed in the PR department of a large hotel chain when she had come into contact with Customs officers from the Investigation Division who were working a trace along the South Coast. She had helped them with their enquiries and had become interested in Customs and Excise – and Chris Lucas – as a result. The romance which had developed had survived despite the distance which often separated them; Chris was based in London and had a flat there. It had been weeks since they had last seen one another.

'Chris is a good man,' said Caines. 'Return my regards, won't you?'

'You may see him tomorrow, sir. He's coming down from London.'

'I'll try to make a point of it. Goodnight.'

A car pulled up outside the house. Tom was in bed, but he had not slept since retiring three hours ago. Turning over, he glanced at the bedside clock. It was two-thirty.

Presently the bedroom door opened quietly and Sue entered. She went to the dressing table and began to remove her jewellery.

'I know you're awake,' she said to Tom without turning.

'Yes,' he said. 'At two-thirty.'

He rose and went into the bathroom to fetch himself a glass of water. Emerging, he noticed the gold coin which Sue had put down on the dressing table, lying in the swathe of light from the doorway.

'What's that?' he asked.

'What do you think it is?'

He picked it up and made to remove the coin from its plastic sheath.

'Don't do that,' Sue said to him. 'Every time it's handled it loses a bit of its value.'

'Where did you get it? This is worth four hundred pounds.'

'As much as that? Well, well.'

'We can't afford to spend that kind of money.'

'Don't worry. It was a gift.'

'A gift? Who from?'

'Does it matter?'

'It matters to me!'

'There's no need to shout, Tom.'

'Who gave it you?'

'Charles Thieron.'

Tom was silent for a moment, staring at her. She turned back to the mirror.

'What's so wrong?' she said. 'He can afford it. I brought him luck, so he bought me a coin.'

'A Krugerrand! Bought it? Where did he buy it?'

Sue's patience was wearing thin. 'In the casino, stupid.'

'Who did he buy it from?'

'How would I know?'

'Who, Sue?'

She rounded on him. 'Listen, I suffer your boring shop talk, I tolerate your stubbornness, and I've even come to accept the fact that you seem to have no interest in what I do – except when it suits you. But there's no way I'm going to allow your work to interfere with my life. Is that clear, Tom?'

'This little present might –'

'Back off. I mean it.'

But Tom was adamant. 'Give it back to him.'

'What?'

'You heard me.'

'No. I won't.'

Tom tossed the coin back on to the dressing table. 'Then accept the consequences.'

'Don't be so pathetic.'

'I mean it, Sue.'

Sue's anger gave way to a smile. 'You're jealous.'

'I want you to return that coin to Thieron. Tomorrow.'

'I damn well won't.'

At nine o'clock the following morning, Tom sat in the office of Harry Caines. Caines had asked to see him, but Tom was not in the best of moods for a chat with his Surveyor.

'You know John Bryce is retiring soon,' Caines remarked. 'Interested in moving over into Excise?'

Tom was surprised by the suddenness of Caines's proposition.

'I might consider it,' he said cautiously.

'Good. It would give you that much more relevant experience.'

'And fit into your plans, sir?'

'Yes. That, too.'

'And which reason has priority?'

'They have equal weight,' Caines told him in a level tone.

'Your offer has my future in mind?'

'Yes, Tom. It makes sense. Think about it, and let me know.'

Tom rose from his chair and made to leave.

'You look tired,' Caines remarked. 'Late night?'

Tom nodded. Then he paused. 'Have you got a moment, sir?'

'Of course.'

'I'd like this to be off the record – at least initially.'

'All right.'

Tom explained about his wife's visit to the casino the previous night and the Krugerrand which Thieron had given her. Caines seldom revealed much through his expression, but Tom could tell he was very interested.

'And this Krugerrand,' he said, 'it's still in your wife's

possession?'

'Yes,' said Tom.

Caines pondered. 'Having been sold at the casino, it's a fair assumption that VAT hasn't been paid on it, wouldn't you say?'

'That's why I brought it up, sir.'

'Could be very delicate, Tom – one way or another.'

'Yes.'

'How many coins a week would make this kind of operation worthwhile?'

'Well, avoiding VAT and assuming a five per cent profit, the seller would make twenty pounds a coin. Sell ten in a week and you have two hundred pounds tax free.'

Caines nodded. 'Well worth the trouble. And Thieron gave it to your wife, eh? If it came to the crunch, would she be a witness?'

Tom was silent. He shook his head.

Caines said nothing for a moment, and Tom had the vague feeling that he had betrayed Sue.

'Granted the delicacy of the situation,' said Caines, 'have you told me everything?'

'Everything that applies to me as a Customs officer, yes.'

'All right, Tom. There's nothing much we can do at the moment. Let's keep our ears to the ground and see what we can pick up.'

Tom headed for the door.

'One more thing,' said Caines.

'Yes?'

'Thanks for letting me know.'

It was apprentices' afternoon at Kalman's salon, and the place was filled with customers taking advantage of cut-price rates. Among them was Alyson, who had decided to have her hair done for Chris's visit.

Her hair had just been washed and she was waiting for the apprentice to return and begin cutting it when she noticed Joseph Kalman in the mirror. He had been moving among his patrons and dispensing professional chatter, but at that moment he paused rather longer at the chair of an attractive woman in her thirties, and Alyson saw him remove several gold coins in plastic sachets and exchange them with the woman for a fat brown envelope. Then he quickly moved on.

Interesting, thought Alyson, at the same time becoming aware that water from her wet hair had begun to trickle down her neck.

Charles Thieron was having an evening drink with friends in the bar of the Yacht Club when Tom Gibbons entered and approached him.

'A word with you,' he said immediately.

His tone was not friendly. Thieron said, 'Now?'

'Please.'

Thieron excused himself from his companions, then followed Tom over to a quiet corner of the bar.

Tom came straight to the point: 'I believe you gave Sue a Krugerrand last night.'

'Yes. That's correct.'

'A bit extravagant, wasn't it?'

Thieron's eyes narrowed. 'Not in my opinion, no.'

'Well it is in mine.'

'There's no need to take offence, Tom. She brought me luck.'

'Well, if she ever brings you luck again, Mr Thieron, please don't let your gratitude become absurd.'

Thieron controlled his temper. 'That's very presumptuous, Tom.'

'Just stating a fact, Mr Thieron. I hope I haven't offended you.'

'I doubt that you could, Mr Gibbons, operating at your level.'

He turned and walked back to his companions at the bar.

# *Chapter Seven*

Next day Tom was sitting with the others in the rest room at the Custom House during their mid-morning break. Caines had taken a few hours off to move his few belongings from the 'Lotus' to his new flat, but he was expected in shortly.

Bruce Tomlin was telling an anecdote about an unexpected passenger he had encountered in the Dutch barn office: 'So I said, "What do you mean you've come from South Africa?" "Hitchhiked," he told me, "via Lagos and Rome." "Oh yes," say I. "Then how come you're aboard a lorry from Barcelona?" Total confusion from the lad for a moment. "Amnesia," he said.'

Everyone laughed.

'Stoned out of his skull,' said Calvin. 'Wouldn't mind joining him.'

Tom said, 'You've only been in charge of the EPU for two days.'

'And nine million forms don't forget.'

'I've had an offer to go over to Excise.'

'Interested?'

'Sort of.'

'Changed your mind about Caines?' asked Bruce.

Tom smiled. 'I'd see more of Alyson in Excise. Like the new haircut, Aly.'

'I'm confused,' said Nigel. 'Who's the haircut for, Aly? Thomas or Chris?'

'Chris,' said Alyson.

Nigel turned to Bruce. 'Nothing like playing the field, is there?'

Alyson and Bruce exchanged glances, both of them finally grasping Nigel's innocent misunderstanding.

'Dangerous pastime, Nigel,' said Bruce.

'Anyway,' said Nigel, 'your hair looks smashing, Aly.'

'Ought to. Best place in town – Kalman's. I had it done on the cheap – apprentices' afternoon. And guess what I happened to see while I was there? Pieces of eight changing hands.'

'What?' said Tom.

'Gold coins, Tom. Krugerrands. Think it's worth reporting to Caines?'

'Yes,' Tom said urgently. 'I know he'll be interested.'

Nigel, seated beside the window, said, 'Here he is now.'

Caines was climbing the stone stairs. Tom bustled Alyson out into the corridor as he entered.

'We'd like to have a word with you, sir,' he said.

Caines looked surprised. But he nodded and led them into his office.

Alyson explained what had happened at the salon.

'Are you sure it was Kalman?' Caines asked.

Alyson nodded. 'I saw him slip the coins into a woman customer's hand. She gave him a brown envelope in return.'

'Well, well,' said Caines. 'How very interesting. Thanks for letting me know, Alyson.'

She departed, but Tom lingered.

'Before this goes any further, sir, you ought to know that I've been to see Thieron.'

Caines studied him. 'Was that wise?'

'I kept it to purely domestic matters.'

'He knows you're in Customs?'

'Yes. But I can assure you that my job didn't enter into our conversation.'

Caines looked as if he was doing mental arithmetic.

'All right, Tom,' he said finally. 'I think I'd better pop upstairs and see the VAT Surveyor.'

Tom left, and Caines rang Jim Benson's extension. Benson, a gruff but cheerful man in his fifties, agreed to see him immediately.

Caines climbed the stairway to the top floor where the VAT people worked.

'Harry,' said Jim Benson as Caines entered his office, 'you come to a deadly boring sea of calm. So no waves, please.'

Caines smiled and shut the door behind him. Benson tapped a calendar on the wall. 'A couple more months and I'm away for ever. So what's all this about?'

'A little query,' said Caines.

'Little? I can hear the rumblings you've caused below right up here.'

'Stop exaggerating.'

Benson motioned for Caines to sit down. 'So?'

'Kalman,' said Caines. 'Joseph Kalman.'

Benson went to a cabinet and removed a file which he brought back to his desk.

'He's registered as a hairdresser, trading under his own name.'

'Does he disclose any other business?'

'No. But let's check the record of visits.' He flipped through the file and perused a page. 'No ancilliary business. Why?'

'He might be expanding a bit. Being a bit naughty.'

'Oh? You want me to organize a visit?'

'Not quite.'

'The man keeps a very tidy set of accounts. No problems. What have you got in mind?'

'Bruce Tomlin, one of my EOs –'

'The academic who's into marine grasses?'

Caines nodded. 'He's had VAT experience.'

'You want Tomlin to do a VAT visit on Kalman?'

'Yes.'

'Aren't you carrying this team idea of yours a bit far?'

'If you're agreeable to me using Tomlin, it would be a help.'

'How long ago was he in VAT?'

'Three years. Plymouth.'

Benson let out a resigned sigh. 'All right, Harry – but on one condition. You go along as well.'

'Why?'

'To supervise.'

'Supervise?'

'So if anything goes wrong, I'm off the hook and you're on it.'

Caines returned Benson's smile. 'Done,' he said, rising.

'Aren't you going to tell me more about Kalman?' Benson asked.

'He may be dabbling in Krugerrands and I'm a bit concerned that it could have implications for one of my staff.'

'Sounds sticky.'

'It could be. Thanks for your cooperation, Jim. I'll go and break the good news to Bruce.'

'Give Kalman fair notice, won't you?'

'Why?'

'For the good name of this department, of course. Who loves the VAT man?'

'Twenty-four hours?'

'If Kalman agrees. That's the absolute minimum, Harry.'

'I won't push it.'

Benson gave another long-suffering smile. 'That's not what I hear.'

Caines went downstairs and summoned Bruce to his office. Bruce was mildly astounded to hear that he was going to make a VAT visit for the first time in three years. But he was a phlegmatic man who had anticipated that Caines's new broom would mean a change in his own working patterns. Returning to the Long Room, he immediately rang Kalman's home number Kalman himself answered.

'VAT office here, Mr Kalman,' said Bruce. 'I wonder when it would be convenient for us to visit?'

'How time flies,' came the reply. 'My turn's come round

again, has it. When do you suggest?'

Kalman sounded perfectly relaxed, so Bruce said, 'What about tomorrow?'

'That's very short notice, isn't it?'

'Yes, I realize that. If it's at all inconvenient I'll happily fix another appointment with you.'

Bruce's politeness paid off, for Kalman said, 'Makes no difference to me. Only too glad to help out. Tomorrow's as good as any other day. Get it over with, eh?'

'Would eleven A.M. be all right?'

'Yes, I think I can manage that.'

'Eleven it is, then. Thank you, Mr Kalman.'

Bruce hung up. Alyson was sitting at the desk opposite, staring at him. She had overheard his side of the telephone conversation.

'You doing a VAT visit?' she asked.

Bruce nodded.

'Our Mr Caines isn't wasting his time, is he? Why the rush to get it done?'

Bruce shook his head. 'Don't ask difficult questions. I've got to go somewhere quiet and bone up on my glory days in VAT.'

When Caines and Bruce arrived at the salon the following morning, Kalman was waiting for them. He led them upstairs to his flat, and sat patiently while Bruce went through his accounts. He's calm, thought Caines: sure of himself. Caines stared around the overfurnished flat as he waited. The room was dominated by an ornate Georgian pedestal desk which stood beside the door. Decor reflects the man, Caines thought, and it was clear to him that Kalman liked to lead a life of conspicuous luxury.

'This is the first time two of you have come along,' Kalman remarked.

'Sometimes the work is supervised,' Caines told him.

'Makes sense.' Kalman was convivial, perfectly at ease.

'You won't find anything to concern you, gentlemen.'

'I'm glad to hear it. Is hairdressing your only business, Mr Kalman?'

'Yes, it is, Mr Caines.'

Arriving at the Custom House after lunch to work his shift, Tom encountered Caines in the corridor.

'Nothing at Kalman's,' Caines told him. 'His books are in good shape, and of course he denies any ancilliary business.'

Tom nodded fatalistically. He had left home with a reminder from Sue about the imminent lunch date with her father. She had been utterly unimpressed when he had told her about his move to Excise, even though he had pointed out that it would mean less overtime. She was still determined that he would end up working for her father. He felt pressurized, harassed.

'So where do we go from here?' he asked.

'For the moment there's nowhere we can go. I'd like you to keep clear of Mr Thieron, Tom. And try to make sure that your wife doesn't receive any more – gifts of that sort.'

Again Tom bristled; he felt like a schoolboy getting a warning from his headmaster. He said, 'I've already made that point to her, sir.'

Then he walked off.

# *Chapter Eight*

Friday morning. Nigel and Bruce were in uniform and had stopped off at the Long Room to pick up their cases before they went on to the ferry terminal.

'VAT yesterday,' Nigel said to Bruce, 'Customs today. Superman Tomlin.'

'Easy when you know how,' said Bruce.

'With all this chopping and changing we'll end up in a shambles.'

'You will. I won't. I think Caines may well make us all more efficient.'

'You do?'

Bruce nodded. 'He's got ability, ambition, and he's totally committed to his career – to the exclusion of everything else.'

'Sounds like you're saying he's obsessive.'

'Not exactly. I think he may be filling the spaces in his life.'

'Spaces? What sort of spaces?'

'Spaces.'

Nigel looked confused. 'You've read far too many botany books for me, Bruce.'

'I'm running a trial tonight.'

'Grasses? I'm playing tennis.'

Sue Gibbons had insisted on a rematch after Nigel had only narrowly beaten her, and he was more than happy to give her another chance.

Calvin Sampson entered the Long Room. 'Do you think the ferry's going to heave to and wait until you pair get to the terminal?'

Bruce picked up his case. 'We're on our way, Cal.'

Calvin watched them leave, then returned to the HEO office. Tom Gibbons was seated at his desk.

'Accepted the transfer into Excise?' Calvin asked.

'Yes,' Tom replied without looking up from the register he was studying.

'Oh, my good old steadfast mate. What price unity now?'

'I don't know what you're moaning about. You're back on the launch today, aren't you?'

'And thank the Lord for it, too. Harbour's heaving with talent this morning. New season – fresh and lovely.'

Tom did not respond.

'Anything wrong?' Calvin asked.

Tom shrugged. 'Lunch with my father-in-law today.'

'Lucky you.'

'That's a matter of opinion.'

'Light one today,' Nigel remarked as he checked through the list of arrivals in the Customs shed.

'All the more reason for being thorough,' Bruce replied.

The ferry had arrived, and lorries were trundling off it and driving towards the Dutch barn. Soon the first drivers began to filter through. Among them was Dave Chapman.

Bruce took his papers, and glanced at the lorry through the window.

'Empty again, I see,' he said to Chapman.

'Yeah. Let down, wasn't I?'

'Couldn't you hang on for a load?'

'Wife's ill. Had to get home.'

'Any spirits?'

'No.'

'Wine?'

'No.'

'Cigarettes?'

'One carton.'

'Anything else?'

'No.'

'All right,' said Bruce. 'Let's take a look.'

There was an instant's hesitation from Chapman before he shrugged and said, 'Fine.'

The two men went outside to the truck, Bruce taking his case. He spent ten minutes checking the bodywork while Chapman stood by. Then he opened the driver's door and began to rummage in the cabin.

Bruce had had an instinct that Chapman was not being entirely frank with him, and so he was thorough in his search of the cab. But there was nothing unusual to be found.

'OK?' said Chapman as he made to climb down.

Bruce paused at the door and wound down the window. Halfway, it stuck. Bruce put pressure on the winding handle, but the window wouldn't budge further.

He stepped down from the cab and took his screwdriver from his kit.

'Don't bother,' said Chapman. 'It's been like that for months.'

'It's no trouble. I'll save you a bit of maintenance.'

He climbed back into the cab and unscrewed the interior panel of the door. As he was doing so, he was peering at Chapman out of the corner of his eye. The driver was now conspicuously nervous.

Bruce removed the panel. There, in the recess, was a soft leather pouch.

At noon Tom Gibbons left the Custom House and drove east along the waterfront to Wrelling Yacht Club Marina. The marina jutted out into the harbour, and it was crammed with yachts of every description. Tom turned into the car park opposite the Club House.

Inside Jack Langley was waiting for him at the bar. His father-in-law was drinking Chivas Regal, but Tom settled for half a lager. They took their drinks through into the well-appointed dining room, its wood-panelled walls adorned with mariners' instruments and old maps.

'I could put you up for membership here,' Jack remarked as they sat down at their table.

'I don't sail,' Tom replied.

'Neither do I. But there are other advantages.'

'No doubt.'

'Eye on the main chance.'

'Meaning?'

'Alert to every opportunity that presents itself.'

'Not my scene.'

'Oh, come on, Tom. Bright man like you will adapt to it easily. Another drink before we eat?'

Tom shook his head.

Jack Langley summoned a waiter, and they ordered. Tom had a simple steak with a side salad, while Jack opted for smoked salmon followed by a lobster freshly boiled from the restaurant tanks. There was a bottle of Moët and Chandon champagne on the table, but Tom declined to have his glass filled, asking instead for mineral water.

'How's my little girl?' Jack asked him as they ate.

'You might know that better than I do.'

'Oh?'

'Late nights and things.'

'Ah, I see – the casino. Well, you were invited.'

'I had to be up early the next day.'

'My little girl's always loved treats. And I've always enjoyed treating her.'

'Which makes her a bit spoilt, perhaps.'

'Don't you spoil your two?'

'Children are one thing. Sue's an adult.'

'Not to her father, Tom. She's a sparkler, my baby.'

'Oh, yes, she certainly sparkles.'

Jack pointed his fork at Tom. 'And frankly, you're not making enough to keep the stones polished. In fact, when did you last buy her anything?'

'If you're talking about diamonds, Jack – not since her

engagement ring.'

'Well, there you are. Don't you think it's time you started looking after things at home a bit more carefully? Odd thing about the pair of us – we both picked wives very much younger than ourselves. And I can tell you they need a very special sort of treatment. Cosseting. Know what I mean?'

'Like pet poodles?' Tom said acidly.

Bruce, Nigel and Dave Chapman were sitting in the Interview Room of the Customs shed. Chapman's suitcase was on the floor, and the leather pouch sat on the table in front of him.

Bruce picked it up and removed the brown tissue paper from the mouth of the pouch. Then he upended it. Over two dozen Krugerrands spilled out on the table.

Bruce looked up at Chapman. 'When I asked you earlier if you had anything to declare, you mentioned nothing except a carton of cigarettes.'

'I didn't know they were there,' Chapman told him.

'Really? Father Christmas saving on postage, is he?'

'I didn't know they were there.'

Bruce picked up the suitcase from the floor and put it on the table.

'This is your suitcase?' he asked.

'Yes.'

Bruce opened it and rummaged inside. Among Chapman's clothing was a piece of brown tissue paper with a corner missing. Bruce matched the crumpled square from the pouch's mouth to the missing segment.

'How do you explain that?' he asked Chapman.

'I'm not the only one who drives that truck.'

'And you lend your suitcase to other people?'

'Yes.'

'I can check whether anyone else has driven the truck.'

'That's up to you.'

Bruce rose and went out, closing the door behind him. He stood in the empty counter area and began to count silently to one hundred. When the count was complete, he returned to the room.

'I checked, Mr Chapman,' he said. 'No one else has driven your truck.'

'That can't be right.'

'Take your shoes off, please.'

'What?'

'Your shoes.'

'You're joking.'

'Take them off, please.'

Reluctantly Chapman complied.

'Put your feet on the table,' said Bruce.

Again Chapman did as he was asked.

'Mr Markham,' Bruce said to Nigel, 'feel the gentleman's feet, please.'

Nigel looked surprised. He scowled at Bruce and hesitated before finally running his hands over the black nylon socks that Chapman was wearing.

'No coins, Mr Markham?' asked Bruce.

'No coins, Mr Tomlin,' he replied.

Bruce had Chapman remove his leather jacket, and then his shirt. Nigel searched both. Nothing was found.

'Now your trousers, Mr Chapman,' said Bruce.

'If you think –'

'Trousers, Mr Chapman.'

Bruce's tone was polite but very firm. With great reluctance, Chapman stripped down to his lurid red-and-green underpants.

'Look!' he said as Nigel searched his trousers, 'I'm not carrying drugs or anything.'

'But what about these coins?' said Bruce.

'I bought them as a gift.'

'How much did you pay for them?'

'Don't remember.'

'But you have a receipt.'

'Lost it.'

'Ah.'

'You win some, you lose some.'

'Try this one for size, Mr Chapman. Under my powers as an officer of Customs and Excise I'm seizing these gold coins –'

'You can't.'

'– on the grounds that they were concealed in a manner intended to deceive an officer. You are not obliged to say anything unless you wish to do so, but what you say may be put into writing and given in evidence.'

Chapman looked as if he couldn't believe it. 'You arresting me?'

'Yes.'

'You can't.'

'Why not?'

'They're not mine.'

'Then whose are they?'

Chapman was silent. Bruce decided to try another tack.

'You're an owner-driver, aren't you?'

Chapman nodded.

'Truck paid for, is it?'

'Nearly.'

'Costly business.'

'You can say that again.'

'Talking about money, Mr Chapman, do you have any idea of the tax on these coins?'

'How much?'

'About seven hundred pounds. And your truck is liable to seizure.'

Bruce waited a moment, allowing the implications to sink in. Then he said, 'You're carrying them for someone, aren't you?'

'Kalman,' admitted Chapman finally.

'The hairdresser? Joseph Kalman?'

'Yes.'

'And how do you deliver?'

'He's waiting for me now. On the flyover at Junction 5 on the motorway.'

'What I need is a good manager,' Jack Langley told Tom as they sat over coffees at the restaurant table. 'Someone to keep his hands on the reins of my affairs. Someone I can trust. And I believe I can trust you, Tom. You'd make eleven grand a year, plus all the perks you can pick up. I intend expanding my operations by at least twenty-five per cent in the coming year, and someone's got to watch over it. I know we haven't always seen eye to eye, but you are family and you're honest. And I reckon that working together will help us get along better.'

Tom stared at Jack Langley's craggy face – a wily, experienced face. The face of a wheeler-dealer.

'Sue knows all about this?' he asked.

Jack Langley nodded. 'What do you say?'

Tom swallowed a mouthful of coffee. 'The offer's better than I had expected – much better.'

'So? Do you accept?'

'You want an immediate answer, and I know Sue's going to push hard for me to accept. But I've made a life's career in Customs and I need more time to think about it.'

Jack Langley stared at Tom for long moments before nodding.

'Fair enough,' he said. 'But don't take too long, Tom. I won't wait forever.'

Tom rose from the table and departed. He drove straight back to the Custom House. As he entered the building he encountered Harry Caines.

'Ah, Tom,' said Caines, 'I'm glad you're back. I've just had a call from Bruce Tomlin at the Dutch barn. He's picked up a driver trying to smuggle Krugerrands into the country. Joe Kalman's apparently waiting on the motorway for the truck. We'll pick him up, take him back to his flat and do a search.'

Tom followed Caines into his office. 'Have you got a warrant?'

'No time for that. I'll use the Writ.'

Caines had gone to the safe which stood beside the window. He opened it and produced a document – the Writ, a permanent search warrant which Customs officers could use in emergencies to search for customed goods.

'Any complications?' Tom asked.

He was thinking of Sue's oblique involvement in the Krugerrand business. Caines knew this.

'None,' he said. 'Kalman's the man we have to deal with.'

Tom nodded, relieved. 'Let's use the Jag. Good impression and all that.'

'Fine. But no high-speed chases if we can help it.'

They drove out of Wrelling, and presently turned on to one of the approach roads to the motorway. Caines spotted Kalman sitting in his Alfa Romeo convertible on the flyover. The hood was down on the car.

Tom approached slowly, and pulled in in front of the Alfa Romeo to forestall Kalman should he attempt a swift getaway.

But Kalman was calmness itself as Caines got out of the Jaguar and walked over to him.

'Well, well,' he said. 'You again. Don't tell me I have a VAT rebate due.'

'May I join you, Mr Kalman?' asked Caines.

'Sure.'

Caines opened the car door and climbed into the passenger seat.

'Admiring the view?' he asked Kalman.

'Taking a breather before getting on to the motorway. You know what it's like.'

'Indeed. Of course I might be able to save you a journey.'

'Oh?'

'Avoid all the hassle down there, I mean. In fact, why don't we go to your place right now?'

Kalman stared at him, still calm. 'You want your hair done?'

Caines did not smile. 'I want to search your premises.'

If Kalman was surprised, he did not show it. 'You need a warrant for that, don't you?'

'I have one, Mr Kalman.' He produced the Writ. 'The language is a bit old-fashioned, but it allows me to search your premises and flat. Shall we go?'

Kalman said nothing for a moment. He stared at the Writ but did not attempt to take it from Caines and examine it. Finally he shrugged and started up the car.

Tom followed them as they drove back to the salon. Kalman parked his convertible at the front of the building and got out. By now he was quietly fuming but still keeping his temper under control. Tom followed Caines into the salon.

The place was busy, but Tom and Caines conducted a thorough search with as much politeness as they could muster. Assistants and customers looked on as they checked through drawers and shelves and work surfaces and cupboards. When asked what was going on, they merely answered that they were Customs officers conducting an official search of business premises; they did not elaborate.

Kalman, now seething, stood watching them. He would not speak to anyone, waving their queries away. Finally Caines announced himself satisfied.

'Now what?' said Kalman.

'Now we search your flat, Mr Kalman,' said Caines.

The three of them went upstairs. Kalman took a bottle of vodka from the drinks cabinet and poured himself a long shot which he did not dilute. He slumped in an Art Deco armchair as Caines and Tom went through bureaux and dressers and stereo cabinets and bookcases. The search took over an hour, but they found no Krugerrands.

Kalman's patience was finally at an end. 'Well, Mr

Caines, you've disturbed my trade, upset my staff, rummaged through all my private belongings. Now what else can I do for you?'

'For the time being,' said Caines, 'nothing, Mr Kalman. I'm extremely sorry if your staff and customers are upset.'

'Then that's it?'

'Yes, Mr Kalman. That's it.'

Kalman strode over to the door and flung it open. 'Then perhaps you'd like to get the hell out of here and leave me in peace.'

Tom was visibly disappointed that they had found nothing. But Caines motioned to him to leave. As they moved towards the door, however, Caines paused and said, 'My father had one just like that.'

Kalman was swallowing a mouthful of vodka.

'Like what?' he said.

Caines indicated the desk beside the door. 'George II, isn't it? You searched the drawers, Tom, did you?'

Tom nodded.

'I remember him telling me, my father, that these kind of desks had lots of secret compartments. Did you check them out, Mr Gibbons?'

Tom frowned, obviously unaware that any such compartments had existed.

Caines walked over to the desk and began examining it.

'Now, where were they?' he mused aloud, his hand sliding under the desk-top. 'If I remember correctly, they're generally – ah, here we are.'

He had pulled out a hidden drawer which was disguised as a panel. Delving into it, he produced a small metal strongbox.

Kalman looked as if he had just swallowed a ferret. Caines smiled pleasantly and said, 'Would you be so kind as to unlock this, Mr Kalman.'

The hairdresser did nothing for a moment. He looked at Tom, then at Caines, as if weighing up the odds. Finally he reached into the inside pocket of his jacket and produced a small key. Caines could see his hands trembling slightly as he unlocked the box.

Caines took it from him, lifted the lid and upended the box on the desk. A pile of Krugerrands tumbled out.

'Mr Kalman!' said Caines with mock outrage and surprise.

# *Chapter Nine*

Chris Lucas stood at the kitchen window of Alyson's cottage and watched her ride her horse around the paddock. Alyson had built several fences for Thomas to jump, and the five-year-old chestnut gelding negotiated them effortlessly.

It was late on a Sunday morning, and Chris, a fair-headed man in his mid-thirties, was preparing lunch. He had arrived from London the previous day, and Alyson had greeted him with the news that she had won her class in the local horse-jumping competition, which qualified her for the County Show. If she won that, the next step would be the Foxhunter at Wembley.

Chris had news of his own, but he was waiting his moment. He returned to the steaks which he was frying. Presently the meal was ready. Chris went to the window and opened it. His timing was good: Alyson had just dismounted from Thomas.

'Grub's up,' he called to her.

'Be with you in a minute,' she replied, leading Thomas towards his box.

Chris turned the steaks and mushrooms on to a plate, then added creamed potatoes and the special salad which he had prepared. Alyson entered, hot and sweaty. She washed quickly under the cold-water tap, then joined him at the table.

'This looks super,' she said to him. 'I don't manage to do much cooking for myself.'

'No,' said Chris. 'Thomas gets all your attention, doesn't he?'

'Quite right, too.'

Chris produced a bottle of French red wine. 'This is special, too. All the way from London.' He uncorked it and poured two glasses. 'A special wine for a special occasion.'

'Oh?' said Alyson, taking her glass. 'How come it's so special?'

'I've got a transfer down here to the local unit.'

She simply stared at him. 'I thought you were happy in London.'

'I was. But I'll be more contented here. Aren't you pleased? It means we can see more of one another.'

Alyson broke into a smile. 'Chris, I'm delighted.'

'There's more. What do you say to us getting married?'

'Married?'

'You know – walk up the aisle, ring on the finger. That sort of thing.'

'When?'

'In the next few months, I thought.'

'This is a bit sudden.'

'I like to catch you unawares. What do you say?'

She considered. 'We'll toast your transfer. I need time to think about the other.'

Chris had expected as much. 'At least give me a definite maybe.'

Alyson looked serious for a moment; then she laughed. 'All right, you've got it.'

They attended to their meal, and the talk turned to Harry Caines. Chris told her about the death of his wife and children, but he wasn't able to add many details to what Bruce Tomlin had already gleaned.

'Have you known him long?' Alyson asked.

'Off and on for quite a few years – but not really. Very few people do know him.'

For afters, Chris produced a blackcurrant crumble still warm from the oven. They ate it with fresh cream and afterwards slumped in an armchair, anticipating a quiet afternoon to themselves. Just then there was a loud tapping on the door.

'Aly?' called a voice. 'Are you in there?'

It was Calvin Sampson. He entered with a buxom blonde on his arm.

'Hello, my lovely,' he greeted her. 'Just passing by. This is Betsi. And you must be Chris Lucas.'

The introductions were performed, with Calvin in his most irrepressible mood. 'Delighted to meet you at last,' he told Chris. 'Betsi, say hello to Christopher Lucas. Sadly he got to Aly before I did. But never mind – you'll do.'

Betsi did not take offence at this remark; she obviously knew that Calvin was incorrigible. Calvin opened the box he was carrying and produced four herring. Two bottles of wine appeared from the pockets of his anorak. He took them into the kitchen.

'Cal,' said Alyson, 'what are you doing?'

'Preparing lunch, my lovely. Betsi, I hope you can cook as good as you look.'

Alyson and Chris could do nothing but stand by with bemused grins as Calvin began to organize their kitchen.

'Chris is transferring down here,' Alyson remarked to him.

'That's funny,' said Calvin. 'I'm thinking about a transfer myself.'

'Where to?' asked Chris.

'Haven't the foggiest yet. But I reckon I've got to get out. This new man Caines has got us all running in circles. I could turn up in the morning and he's likely to say, "Sampson, my man, go and raise the *Titanic*." Must be an easier life somewhere. God, Betsi, I'm starving. Get those fish frying, will you?'

Monday morning. Nigel sat at his desk, humming to himself as he attended to some paperwork.

'You're cheerful this morning,' Alyson remarked.

But as he reached for a document wallet, Nigel winced

and grasped his arm.

'I think I'm getting tennis elbow,' he said.

The internal telephone rang, and Alyson took the call.

'Mr Caines wants to see you,' she informed Nigel.

Nigel went down the corridor to the Surveyor's office, wondering what he had done wrong this time. But Caines was friendly enough.

'Ah, Nigel,' he said. 'That seizure of Spanish brandy.'

'Yes, sir?'

'It must be destroyed today. Nice little job for you.'

Nigel nodded. 'Now, sir?'

'No. I'll let you know. I have to be there with you, don't I? We'll do it later.'

'Later' was that afternoon. The easiest way of disposing of unwanted liquor was to pour it straight into the public sewer. So Nigel and Caines stacked the crates in the toilet and then began ceremoniously emptying them down the WC.

'Our country ought to be proud of us, sir,' Nigel remarked. 'None of my friends believe that we actually pour it away.'

'No one does,' replied Caines.

Nigel peered into the bowl. 'I do believe, sir, that it's killing all known germs.'

'It's good brandy, Nigel.'

'This is the last bottle, sir. Shall I do the honours?'

Caines nodded. Nigel poured the contents into the bowl, then flushed it. As the liquor drained away, he saluted.

'I keep seeing vineyards, sir.'

Caines smiled. 'And the sound of castanets in your ears?'

'Now you come to mention it, sir.'

'And when you pour vodka away?'

'Sleighbells. And men in fur hats.'

The deed done, they returned to the Long Room. Tom Gibbons had just arrived, along with his wife.

'Good afternoon, sir,' he said to Caines. 'You haven't

met my wife.'

'How do you do, Mrs Gibbons,' Caines said.

Sue put on her most winning smile. 'You must come over for a drink soon, Mr Caines. Tom's been very remiss.'

'That's very kind of you.'

'Excuse me, but I just popped in to see an old school friend.' Now she was looking at Nigel, who was obviously surprised by her appearance. Caines and Tom went out into the corridor.

'I'm sorry, sir,' Tom said. 'She just drove up as I was coming in.'

'Not to worry,' said Caines. He glanced back into the Long Room. 'Unpredictable things, wives.'

Tom departed for his office. As Caines was heading down the corridor, Alyson entered.

'Good afternoon, sir,' she said. 'I thought you might like to know that Chris – Chris Lucas – has got a transfer down here. To the local unit.'

'I'm very glad for you. He'll stay in Investigation?'

'Yes. Would you like to come to dinner this evening, sir? We're celebrating.'

Caines did not immediately reply. Alyson took it as a preamble to a refusal. 'Of course, if you're –'

'No, no. That'll be splendid. Thank you.'

'Very casual. Eat about eight.'

Alyson's cottage was twenty minutes' drive from the centre of Wrelling. It was a small, rather rundown affair, but the two-acre paddock compensated for that as far as Alyson was concerned. Her father, a dairy farmer, had bought her a New Forest pony when she was five, and she had been in love with horses ever since. She had poured most of her savings into buying Thomas and had never regretted it.

Caines arrived on the stroke of seven. Chris Lucas was in the kitchen and Alyson was giving Thomas a brief workout when he arrived. The two men watched her canter the horse around the perimeter of the paddock.

'Very much in control, isn't she?' remarked Caines.

Chris nodded. 'Know anything about horses?'

'Only what I've picked up from Dorian Williams on TV.'

'Same here. I'm having to learn, though.'

'Yes, I can see that would be important. She's serious, isn't she?'

'Very!'

'Could have your hands full down here, then. Reckon you'll adjust to the change of pace?'

'I doubt there'll be that great a change. You heard about that heavy drugs thing up in London?'

Caines nodded. Large quantities of cannabis were being smuggled into the country and ending up in the capital. Caines knew that Chris had been working on the case.

'Well,' Chris said, 'we think Wrelling may be one of the areas involved.'

Caines was not entirely surprised. 'So the move's practical as well as emotional.'

'It's mainly the second. Aly's very important to me.'

'This drugs thing – it could have implications for us, then.'

'Could be. We'll have to wait and see.'

Alyson was now taking Thomas over the fences.

'How good is that horse?' Caines asked.

'It keeps winning and it stays sound.'

'Will it get through . . . Wembley she's aiming for, isn't she?'

Chris shook his head. 'Pie in the sky. Thousands try to qualify for the Foxhunter. Only about forty get through to the final. But if you could do it on dedication alone, Aly'd be there.'

'Yes, that's plain indeed. You're a lucky man.'

'And a good cook, too. You have to be, with Alyson. And it's time I was slaving over a hot stove so that you two can slaver over warm plates.'

* * *

With the aid of a large brandy and an even larger cigar, Jack Langley sat on the verandah of his house, contemplating the glorious flowerbeds and the billiard-table lawns of his garden. His wife appeared, looking elegant and desirable in a long sky-blue dress which hugged her slim contours. She held a cordless telephone.

'It's for you,' she said.

'Tell 'em to call back. I'm having my lunch.'

'Business, darling. I think you should.'

Reluctantly Jack took the phone from her. He listened for a while, then said, 'No, I can't, I've got a meeting at four. . . Well, I'm certainly not ripping up half a mile of tarmac because you didn't keep your eyes open. . . Yes, I'll sort it out from here and I'll sort you out tomorrow morning.'

He slammed the phone down and glared up at Helen. 'Bloody hell – he calls himself a manager. Couldn't manage a riot, if you ask me. And I'm paying him twenty-five grand a year.'

'Which is why you need Tom.'

Jack swallowed a mouthful of brandy. 'I don't think we're going to get him. He's in a rut and won't shift.'

'Then maybe you should try harder. For all our sakes.'

Jack squinted up at her. 'What do you mean?'

'Our little girl is getting very restless. If she walks out on him we could end up with a house full of grandchildren.'

Jack shook his head. 'You've been restless in your time, but you're still here.'

'I've got good reason to be. She hasn't.'

Jack knew what she meant. 'What happened to romance, eh?'

'It's sitting in the bank, darling, where it belongs.'

Jack looked contemplative. 'So what do you suggest?'

'If Tom had a pocketful of money and spent more time with her, then maybe the old flame would be rekindled.

Force his hand, Jack. You're good at that sort of thing.'

Jack looked thoughtful again.

'I hear,' said Helen, 'that he's not getting on too well with his new boss.'

A slow smile fractured Jack's craggy face. 'Now there's a thought.'

He reached for the phone again and punched out the private number of a town councillor whom he knew well.

'Terry Carr,' said a voice.

'Terry, it's Jack Langley. You know the twinning binge we're having tomorrow night, yes? Well, I'd like you to invite the Customs chap.'

'What Customs chap?'

'The new top man, Harry Caines.'

There was a pause. 'Could be difficult, Jack. The invitations have all been posted. And what the hell for? I don't like Customs.'

'Listen, Terry – you owe me. I want Caines to be invited.'

Again there was a pause. Jack knew that Carr would do as he asked, for Carr had had his pocket well lined in exchange for ensuring that Jack obtained planning permission on a number of controversial building projects.

'All right, Jack,' Carr said at last. 'I'll invite him. Funnily enough, I was about to ring you. There's been a change of venue. We're holding it at the home of a Frenchman who's been living here for the past year. He heard about it and offered his house in the cause of Anglo-French relations.'

'Oh?' said Jack. 'What's his name?'

'Charles Thieron. Know him?'

Jack Langley and Charles Thieron stood apart from the rest of the guests at a table holding several bottles of wine. Thieron was drawing a cork from a bottle of Beaune.

'We'll decide which are best,' he was saying, 'and I'll send some crates round to you.'

'Generous,' said Jack. 'You must want something.'

Thieron smiled. 'Perhaps I do have a – what do you say? – ulterior motive. I like it here, so I begin to look around for things to interest me. My European business looks after itself with only occasional help from me, so I'll involve myself here. Perhaps you'd like to make some suggestions.'

'Why not register as a charity?'

Again Thieron smiled. 'I understand. You would rather wait until we are much older friends before you invite me into something. But I make a short-cut and invite myself.'

Jack studied him for a long while.

'How deep do you want to go?' he asked.

'I'll go as deep as necessary,' Thieron told him. 'I have a hatred of limits. Maybe I should say now that I deal mostly in cash. Would this be a problem?'

'No. If I'm able to find something that suits you.'

'Ah, good. I'm so glad we understand one another.'

French and English town officials milled about in the spacious main hall where the reception was taking place. Attractive young women in Thieron's employ were serving drinks and titbits on trays, while more elaborate buffets were spread out on two long tables flanking the guests.

Suddenly a tall man in a dark suit emerged from the crowd and walked over to Thieron and Jack Langley.

'Mr Thieron?' he said.

'Ah . . . yes. Mr. . . ?'

'Caines. Harry Caines. Customs and Excise. I'm the new Surveyor here.'

'Of course. Welcome.'

'It was very generous to offer the Association your house for this reception, Mr Thieron. Such short notice, too.'

Thieron shrugged expansively. 'Twin towns, and therefore a party that is half French, half English. So I won't feel too lost. Have you met Mr Langley?'

Jack Langley offered his hand, pleased that Caines had

fallen into his conversational lap. At this point another guest approached Thieron, drawing him away.

'Part of the Association, Mr Langley?' asked Caines.

'That's right. I'm the treasurer. Always like to be where the money is. And please call me Jack. You and I are practically related, in a manner of speaking.'

'Really?'

'Tom Gibbons. My son-in-law.'

'Oh, I see. I didn't know.'

Caines had not been surprised to receive a telephone invitation to the twinning reception; Surveyors were frequently invited to civic ceremonies. And when he had heard that the reception was to be held at Thieron's house, he had been determined to attend. He had been discreetly watching the Frenchman for the last hour, weighing him up. The man was smooth and very assured, and certainly a person who liked wealth and power. Jack Langley was more of a rough diamond to external appearances, but it was clear that he, too, was wealthy and influential.

'Could do with your opinion,' Jack Langley was saying to him, 'I've made Tom a little offer, to join my business. I think he'll do very well. What do you think?'

Caines peered at him. 'I've no idea what your business is, so I'm scarcely qualified to judge.'

'Development. Leisure Centres at the moment. Plan 'em, build 'em, franchise them off before they open.'

'Ah,' said Caines.

'So what do you think? About Tom?'

'I think I'm even less able to answer your question. Surely it's a family matter?'

'Just wanted your personal reaction.'

'It would be difficult for me to say.'

Jack Langley stared back at him. Then he nodded. 'Understood. Etiquette and all that. But you can tell me what length of notice he has to give.'

'One month, Mr Langley.'

'Well, that'll be fine. Just fine. Thank you, Mr Caines.'

The telephone rang while Tom was at the breakfast table. Sue picked it up in the adjoining room, and Tom found himself trying to listen in on her conversation. But he was not quite able to make out what she was saying.

Presently she appeared in the doorway, pausing there and making a point of looking at him.

'What was all that about?' he asked.

'It was Daddy. He was at a reception last night.'

'Isn't he always?'

'Business, Tom. Harry Caines was there, too. Jack spoke to him. About you.'

Tom stared at her, waiting.

'About the job he's offered.'

Tom could feel himself growing hot with anger. 'Your father discussed that with Caines?'

'Yes. Apparently they had quite a chat. Daddy finds Caines a very interesting man.'

Without a further word, Tom rose from the table and walked out to his car. He climbed in and drove quickly to the Custom House. Entering, he knocked on Caines's door and opened it. Caines was seated at his desk.

'I'd like a few minutes,' Tom said. 'If you can spare them.'

Caines, immediately registering his agitated state, motioned to a chair. Tom closed the door behind him, but he remained standing.

'I understand you spoke to my father-in-law last night, sir.'

'No,' said Caines, guessing what was coming. 'He spoke to me.'

'And discussed me.'

'Certain information was volunteered, yes.'

'I very much object to that, sir.'

'I didn't say by whom it was volunteered.'

'The fact that my name came up at all –'

'Tom.'

'– is very disturbing to me.'

'Tom! Calm down, will you? Let's try facts. The only information I gave was terms of resignation.'

Tom was not mollified. 'Which means you discussed me.'

'Which means I listened. What else could I do? Your father-in-law approached me.'

'He told you about the job offer?'

'Yes.'

'He had no right to.'

'Then take that up with him, Tom. Your future is your own business.'

Tom paused, some of his anger evaporating. 'That's not my understanding of the conversation you had.'

'I did not discuss you,' Caines insisted. 'Of course you're free to believe what you wish.'

Caines was resolutely calm, and now Tom began to feel that he had been hasty.

'I seem to have got it all wrong,' he said. 'Sorry to take up your time, sir.'

He made to leave, but Caines said, 'Tom. Sit down for a moment.'

Tom hesitated, then did so. Caines studied him before letting out a small sigh.

'Teamwork for me,' he said, 'means a kind of loyalty to each other. I don't talk out of turn, and I offer support – true support – to my colleagues. That's my philosophy. I like everything up front, and I dislike manipulation.'

'And you think I'm being manipulated? My father-in-law set me up last night at the reception.'

'That's up to you to decide, isn't it?'

It was Tom's turn to sigh. 'It's really very embarrassing. I'm sorry you got involved.'

'But it's served a useful purpose, don't you think?'

Tom frowned. 'Not that I can see.'

'Start from the fact that you object to the re-organization of this office.'

Tom did not bother to deny it.

'Add to that your own ambitions. You wanted this job of mine, Tom. We both know it.'

'I've never tried to hide it.'

'Which makes you at the least a disappointed man. And possibly a resentful one. Yes?'

'The useful purpose?'

'I'm coming to it. What's happened has made me aware of what's going on and perhaps allows me to say that if you're considering resigning, then really consider it. I'm not trying to force your hand either way. But don't let a misreported chat last night push you into making the wrong decision.'

# *Chapter Ten*

Alone at her desk, Alyson looked thoughtful. Chris was away, and she had not heard from him in the past few days. She knew he was busy with his work and did not like to discuss it with anyone outside his department. But aside from a brief telephone call to tell her that he was in Basingstoke, he had not been in touch and she was annoyed with him.

Calvin entered. He, too, was somewhat morose. Letting out a long sigh, he said, 'I'm back to those bloody forms tomorrow.'

'No more trips around the harbour?' said Alyson.

'No. I think I ought to put in for a transfer.'

'Don't be daft, Cal. You'll perk up.'

Calvin looked dubious. At this point Chris himself walked into the Long Room.

'Where have you been?' Alyson asked immediately.

'Working,' he told her.

'You might have got in touch.'

'It wasn't possible.'

'Oh, come off it.'

'Honest. It's a big'un, the job I'm on. I'm heading back to London. Called in to see you.'

'And I'm supposed to be grateful.'

'Come on, Aly. You know what it's like.'

'Do I? I don't want details, Chris, but you ring me from Basingstoke – then nothing. If you can't trust me. . .'

'It isn't that.'

'Oh, yes it is. You people in Investigation have some mystique about secrecy.'

Chris was clearly surprised by her irritation. 'I thought you'd understand.'

'Not being taken for granted I don't.'

'Listen, Aly, I've really got to go.'

'Go then.'

But she relented a little, allowing him to give her a kiss before he departed.

The bedside clock showed five minutes to midnight. Sue Gibbons sat in bed, reading *Cosmopolitan*. She looked up at Tom as he emerged from the bathroom.

'How long are you going to sulk?' she asked. 'It's gone on for days.'

Tom, in a white towelling bathrobe, said nothing.

'I think you're behaving like a child,' she added.

'You should know all about that.'

'Oh,' she said, feigning hurt. 'A barb. I must be making progress.'

'Indifference I can just about take, Sue. But not lies. You and your father. God, he must think I'm stupid.'

'Is that why he's offered you a job?'

'You know he spoke to Caines at the reception. Were you in on it?'

'"In on it"? As a matter of fact, I wasn't. But there's always another time.'

'Meaning?'

'You really need it spelled out, don't you? All right, let's spell it out then.' She sat up further in bed, glaring at him. 'I can see no point whatsoever in you stumbling along on tuppence a year in a dreary job where they don't even think you're fit for promotion. And with people who nick other people's presents.'

Tom stared back at her. 'Meaning Thieron's gold coin?'

'It was a gift, Tom. To me.'

'A stupid gift. Customs were within their rights to seize it.'

To his surprise, Sue did not attempt to argue the point. Instead she changed tack: 'I also don't see why we shouldn't have a bit more fun than we're having now. Jack's job would give us that. So why are you being so stubborn about it?'

'Has it ever occurred to you that your idea of fun might be different from mine?'

'Yes,' she said pointedly. 'Yes, it has, Tom. And that's what bothers me.'

Harry Caines sat in his living room, listening to Mozart on his stereo cassette player. Around him stood several cardboard boxes, containing his belongings. From one, he removed a family photograph which had been carefully wrapped in newspaper. It showed a woman and two young children. Reverently he placed it on the sideboard and stared at it for a moment before delving into a carrier bag and removing a loaf of bread. He took it into the kitchen, then went to the fridge and removed a tub of soft margarine, a few slices of ham and a carton of orange juice.

Caines prepared the sandwiches with a minimum of fuss, then took them over to the window and stared out at the town quay and the dark waters of the harbour. Cars passed by on the quayside road, and the white masts of moored yachts rocked gently in the swell. He returned his gaze to the photograph and almost absent-mindedly bit into one of the sandwiches as Mozart played on.

'Sue, my dear,' said the voice of Charles Thieron. 'How are you?'

Sue cradled the receiver in the well of her shoulder. 'Having a late breakfast in bed, actually, Charles.'

'Have you spent your little gold coin yet?'

'Of course not. I sleep with it under my pillow.'

'Lucky little coin. Listen, my darling, I have been let down most horribly and in my need I turn to you.'

She smiled into the phone. 'Florence Nightingale at your service.'

'Who is this?'

'Oh, an English do-gooder. Not really my type.'

'Ah. Well, my problem: I am taking a little party to Cherbourg tomorrow and my hostess has let me down. I am on my knees begging you to take her place.'

Again Sue was amused. 'Charles, you must get up at once. It's so undignified.'

'Then you will help? The forecast is good for the next twenty-four hours. There is a ridge of high pressure moving up the Channel. The weather will be perfect.'

Sue came to an immediate decision. 'I'll be there. What time?'

'Seven sharp at the marina. You will bring Tom if he is free?'

It was more a query than a request – a necessary courtesy.

'He's never free,' Sue said. 'I'll come alone.'

There was a pause, and then Thieron said, 'Good. I look forward to it.'

He rang off. Sue put the phone down, then considered. She punched out her parents' number. When the maid answered, she asked for her mother.

'Good morning, Sue,' Helen Langley said presently.

'Morning, Helen. Guess what? Charles Thieron has invited me to take a trip to Cherbourg on his launch tomorrow.'

'Has he now? Are you going?'

'I'd be a dope not to, wouldn't I?'

'What about Tom?'

'Be a waste of breath mentioning it to him. Path of duty and all that. But he'd be livid if he thought I was going on my own. I need an alibi. Any ideas?'

Helen gave a small laugh. 'I should be disapproving, but I can't say I blame you.' She considered. 'Tell him you've got toothache and I've arranged an appointment for you with my Canadian man in London.'

'He'll complain about the expense.'

'Tell him I'm paying. What time are you leaving?'

'I have to be there by seven.'

'Then say the appointment's for nine, so you have to leave early.'

'Sounds good. Watertight, in fact. You used that one yourself?'

Helen tut tutted. 'Now that would be telling.'

'What is this job you're working on?' Alyson asked Chris.

They lay in bed at Chris's flat in London. Chris had telephoned her the previous day and apologized for his absences before insisting that she drive up to London and spend her day off with him. He had cooked a splendid meal for them, and they had spent the evening making love and reaffirming their commitment to one another.

Chris stared at her in the darkness. 'I can't give you all the details, but it's cannabis. In vast quantities.'

She waited.

'Ends up here in town, of course. But it's coming in on the coast somewhere.'

'The ferries?'

'We don't think so. These are big-time boys.'

'Our area?'

'Not necessarily. It's a long coast. And in some ways the transfer point is incidental. The crisis is here in London, and I don't want to leave until we've exploited it to the full.'

'Exploited it?'

'There's some kind of split between the suppliers. The big men are getting rough with one another.'

'Sounds nasty.'

'May be useful, though. I'm hoping to find a way of driving the wedge even deeper. Bust them wide open.'

After-lunch brandies were being served on the sun-deck of Charles Thieron's launch as it ploughed its way across the Channel. Sue Gibbons lay on the deck with two other women called Kiki and Fiona, who looked like models from the pages of *Vogue*. With them was Thieron and another man called Bob. Both Kiki and Fiona were topless, and Sue was wondering whether she should remove the bra of her white polka-dot bikini. Meanwhile Fiona was in the middle of an anecdote:

'So there we were up this tree picking pineapples and dropping them on poor old George's head. He was so pissed he just kept saying "Bloody monkeys!"' Fiona waited for laughter, then continued: 'And then he would insist on flying his own plane everywhere. God, I know now why it's called island-hopping! It was a nightmare, I can tell you. Like an old World War One movie.'

Another man had come within earshot of their group.

'How's your little Cessna, Harold?' Bob asked him.

'Grounded, I'm afraid. Waiting for parts. Damn nuisance, because Elton's in Monserrat and it's open house if we could get there.'

'Ah,' said Thieron lazily. 'The Caribbean. . .'

'Do you know Antigua?' Fiona asked Sue.

'Er . . . no. I've been to Jamaica.'

Kiki looked shocked. 'Oh, it's so touristy there.'

'Well,' Sue said hastily, 'that was ages ago. With Daddy.'

'I can't *bear* sharing a beach.'

'No?' said Bob.

Fiona smiled at him. 'I'd make an exception for you, darling.'

'Where *do* you go?' Kiki asked Sue.

Sue felt out of her depth. Hesitantly she said, 'We went to Crete last summer.'

Kiki and Fiona said nothing, but their expressions indicated that they considered Crete positively old hat.

Thieron came to Sue's rescue: 'Sue has this martinet of a husband – work, work, work.'

Fiona made a sound which managed to be both sympathetic and condescending. 'Such a tiresome word, isn't it?'

Presently the girls stretched out on towels to sunbathe

while the men lounged in deck chairs. Sue removed her bra top, but she lay demurely on her front. Beside her a cork popped.

She sat up, tying her bra back on. Thieron was pouring champagne into two glasses, his eyes on her.

'Don't you want to bronze all over?' he asked.

'I think there'd be a few questions from Tom.'

Thieron merely smiled. Sue took the proffered glass from him.

It was a hot day, and the launch made steady but gentle progress across the Channel. Overhead the sky was a flawless blue. Fiona fell asleep, and Kiki's eyes were closed as Harold smoothed sun-lotion into her chestnut-brown back. Sue, too, closed her eyes, wrapped in blissful warmth. Thieron and Bob were sitting nearby in a double sun-rocker, and occasionally their voices carried to her. It was mainly small talk, but her ears pricked as she heard Bob say, 'How big is your share now?'

'Sharing, my dear Bob, no longer interests me.'

'What do you mean, Charles? Have you bought them out?'

'No need. We are having a little war instead.'

The launch arrived in Cherbourg harbour shortly before noon. After dropping anchor, a dinghy was lowered. Sue and Thieron stood together on the deck, waiting for Kiki and Fiona, who had gone below to dress for the journey ashore.

'Perhaps we can find you a little something to match the coin,' Thieron said to Sue.

She smiled at him. 'You mustn't spoil me, Charles. It might go to my head.'

Thieron returned the smile. 'I can but hope.'

It was after seven when Tom arrived home from work. He tossed his cap on the hall table and walked into the drawing room. It was empty.

'Sue?' he called, walking back into the hallway. 'You upstairs?'

But it was Connie who appeared on the landing.

'She's not home yet, Mr Gibbons,' she told Tom.

'Bloody long dentist's appointment,' Tom said with a frown.

'I expect she stayed up to do some shopping,' Connie suggested. 'Will you come and see to the children, Mr Gibbons? They're being very naughty and I can't get them to bed.'

Tom swallowed his drink in one. 'Righto, Connie, I'll see to the poor motherless brats.'

He bounded up the stairs, calling out: 'Here comes a candle to light you to bed, here comes a chopper to chop off your head!'

Lanterns were lit on the deck of the launch as it slid through the twilit waters, heading home to Wrelling. Couples swayed to a moody jazz rendition of 'As Time Goes By', holding one another close. Sue Gibbons, in a long midnight-blue dress, had her arms on the white-jacketed shoulders of Charles Thieron. A new gold pendant hung at her breast, and Thieron regarded it approvingly.

'It looks lovely on you,' he remarked.

'You're spoiling me,' Sue replied.

Thieron shook his head. 'Gratitude. Simply gratitude. It was so good of you to come at my call.'

'Just whistle, as the lady said.'

'Miss Nightingale?'

'Lauren Bacall.'

Thieron's hands were on her waist. 'Have you enjoyed it a little bit?'

'You kidding?'

'This is the sort of life you and Tom could be living.'

For a moment she thought he was going to kiss her.

'I'll remind him,' she said.

# *Chapter Eleven*

'I have always felt,' Charles Thieron remarked, 'that the art of discouragement should tend towards the permanent. That's the point, gentlemen. You did not hit them hard enough, and now it is time to do so.'

Thieron was standing at the snooker table in a basement room of his house. He lined up a red ball and potted it expertly. There was a cone of light over the green baize, but the rest of the oak-panelled room was in semi-darkness. The two men whom Thieron was addressing stood motionless, with their backs to the wall, watching him but saying nothing.

Thieron moved around the table and lined up the black.

'It's time we took them out,' he said. 'Once and for all.' The black thudded into the pocket. 'They are our competitors as long as they have merchandise to sell. Am I not right?'

He had straightened and was regarding the men.

'Well, Frank?' he said to the taller of the two.

'What are you proposing?' asked Frank.

'We use a truck,' Thieron told him, 'Heavy chassis and front bars. You go in through the street window –'

'It's a bloody travel agents, Charles!'

Thieron nodded. 'Great believers in a legitimate front, our rivals. Always were.'

'This is London,' said the other man. 'We're not talking about the Green Belt. The boys in blue would be on the spot in five minutes.'

'And you'll be gone by then, my dear Barry. The moment you cut the ignition it sets the timer going for the present you'll be carrying in the back. You will have three minutes to get out and into the taxi which will then be waiting for you.'

Frank and Barry looked at one another dubiously.

'The Bill have got very humpy about bombs,' Frank said. 'It's Special Branch territory. Could be very dodgy.'

Thieron stared at him coldly. 'Are you telling me you don't want to do it, Frank?'

Frank withered under his stare. 'I never said that. I just meant – well, it won't be easy, that's all.'

'But you'll be well paid, won't you? The two of you?'

Thieron waited until both men had nodded. Then he smiled and leaned over the table once more, lining up his next shot.

'It's all behind the computer terminals,' he told them. 'Along the walls. Rows and rows of it, in little compartments. More grass than a prairie. When that little lot burns, Frank, you're going to get some of the highest firemen in the metropolitan area!'

With a smirk of relish, Thieron send another red ball thudding down a pocket.

'My life is my own,' Sue Gibbons told her husband. 'And it's damn well going to stay that way, OK?'

Tom was at the breakfast table, finishing a cup of coffee while Sue cleared the table around him.

'And I get what's left over, do I?' It was a continuation of the argument they had had the previous night when Sue had come home late. It had not taken her long to admit that she had spent the day on a jaunt to Cherbourg with Charles Thieron. She had been almost proud of the fact.

'You wouldn't have come on the cruise even if you had been free!' Sue said. 'You're never available – on principle.'

Tom sighed. He was tired of their endless arguments, tired of Sue taking every opportunity to show her contempt for him.

But Sue herself was far from finished. 'You don't want me to know anyone, do you? Not in any way that matters?'

'How does anyone get to know Charles Thieron "in any way that matters"? The man's got more faces than Big Ben.'

'How do you know? You haven't even tried to get to know him.'

'He's not my type.'

'Oh, very funny. Is that what passes for humour in the Custom House?'

Tom finished off his coffee and said nothing.

'If you don't like it,' Sue went on, 'why don't you do something about it? All I get from you are moans and sulky silences. You resent practically everything about us – the car, the house, my father.'

'All I ever wanted was a proper wife. And I haven't got that, have I?'

Sue was finally goaded to fury. 'Then go and look for one, damn you! Pack the suitcases I gave you and get out of here! I'm sick of your voice, your job – I'm sick of you, and I wish you'd get the hell out of here!'

She stormed out, slamming the door behind her and leaving Tom in a stunned silence.

Nigel was at his desk in the Long Room when the telephone rang.

'Customs and Excise,' he said. 'Good morning.'

'Just the man I was hoping to speak to,' said the voice of Sue Gibbons. 'How's your tennis elbow, Nigel?'

'It's fine now, Sue. How are you?'

'Could be better. I had a tennis date with a girlfriend this afternoon, but she's had to back out. Fancy standing in? We were going to have a sort of high tea afterwards at the house. The kids are at my mother's, and Tom has a lot of paperwork to catch up on at the office. I'd appreciate the company.'

There was a brief silence, then Nigel said, 'As it happens, I've got the afternoon off.'

'Well, there you are, then. It's Kismet, isn't it?'

'Sorry?'

'Fate, Nigel! What do you say?'

'Sounds good. What time?'

'About two. See you then.'

Nigel put the phone down, aware that Alyson and Bruce, who were sitting nearby, had been half-listening to his conversation. He saw them exchange a glance, but they said nothing. With a conspicuous show of concentration, Nigel returned to his pile of manifests.

'Heard from Chris?' Bruce asked Alyson.

'Not for the last twenty-four hours,' she told him.

'This business in London is keeping him on the move a bit, isn't it?'

Alyson peered at him. 'What have you heard?'

'No more than you, probably. It's under wraps, isn't it?'

She nodded. 'It always is with Investigation. He hasn't said much.'

'Well, perhaps it's better than bringing it home.'

For some reason Alyson felt uneasy with the conversation. In an effort to change the subject, she said, 'I hear your book has reached the – what is it? – "proofs" stage or something?'

Bruce nodded. 'Galley-proofs. You have to check that they've printed what you've actually written. If you miss it first time around they may charge you for altering it later!'

'I can't see you missing anything. Old eagle eyes. Think it'll be a best-seller?'

'Not at fifty-five pounds a copy. And I don't think your average Dick Francis fan is going to be very interested in coastal erosion, do you? Perhaps I ought to come up with a punchier title. Something like *Everything You Need To Know About Grass*.'

'It'd go a bomb with your drug culture,' said Alyson.

* * *

'Yes, Frank,' Charles Thieron said into the telephone, 'I heard all about it. You did a good job, Frank. . . Look, it was an accident. Nobody could have known. It happens. All it means is that there'll be some extra heat for a while. . . No, nobody's going to find the cab. Don't worry, it'll be scrap in twenty-four hours. . . You've got the tickets, so take the night ferry. Everything's arranged the other end.'

Thieron put the phone down and stared at the oil painting on the opposite wall of his drawing room. It showed a lion devouring a lamb. How apt, he thought, pouring himself a celebratory brandy.

Tom Gibbons sat at his desk, trying not to listen to Calvin, who was recounting the details of his latest conquest.

'You know what she said?' Calvin told him. 'You're really into people, aren't you? That's what she said. You're really into people, Calvin.'

'Did you tell her how often?' Tom said.

'She's a very psychic sort of girl, you know. All joss sticks and save the whale. Did you know we all have a third eye, Tom?' Calvin tapped his forehead. 'Somewhere up here. Patty says when it's opened it gives you an entirely different view of the world.'

'What a load of drivel.'

Calvin peered at him, finally gathering that Tom was not in the best of humours.

'Look,' said Tom, 'being bored by your past life is one thing. I've come to see it as an occupational hazard, working here. But having to listen to you anticipating what's to come is pushing it a bit, frankly.'

Calvin looked hurt. 'You never minded before.'

'I was being polite.'

'Were you?' Calvin was stung. 'Were you now? It seems to me, old boy, that there was more than a little of the old extra-curricular interest involved. No need to go blaming me if the conjugal bed isn't living up to –'

'Why don't you learn to shut up, Calvin!'

Both men's tempers had now flared. Tom was still smarting over the latest row with Sue, and he just wanted to be left alone. Calvin, too generous by nature to bear a grudge, immediately relented.

'Sorry, old boy,' he said. 'Talking out of turn.'

'No,' said Tom, 'it's my fault. I'm just a bit on edge.'

'I'm to blame,' Calvin insisted. 'Talk too much. Would you rather I listened? I have been known to manage it at times.'

Slowly Tom smiled. 'I'd bore you to death.'

'Course you would,' Calvin agreed. 'Didn't say I'd enjoy it, did I? What about a drink when we finish tonight?'

Tom indicated the pile of papers on his desk. 'One more day and this lot is going to collapse on me. I'm determined to get it all cleared today, which means working late. But thanks anyway.'

It was three-thirty in the afternoon when Caines's phone rang. He picked up the receiver, saying, 'Caines.' Then his face went slack with shock as the voice at the other end of the line began talking. The message was a brief and devastating one, but Caines was silent for seconds after it had been delivered.

'I understand,' he said finally. 'Thank you for calling me.'

He rose from his desk and went down the corridor to the Long Room. Only Bruce was there.

'Is Alyson back yet?' he asked.

'She and Nigel have the afternoon off,' Bruce reminded him.

'Any idea where she might be?'

'I think she's gone home. Is something wrong, sir?'

Caines shook his head, but it was not a denial.

'I may not be back this afternoon,' he told Bruce. Then he exited.

Caines climbed into the Astra and drove out to Alyson's cottage. When he arrived he saw her in the paddock, taking Thomas over the fences. Alyson spotted him as he was getting out of the car, and she reined in the horse.

Caines walked across the paddock, heedless of the mud. Alyson had dismounted and was holding Thomas's muzzle. On seeing Caines's grim expression, she said, 'What's wrong?'

A white cloth had been draped over the dining table in the drawing room, and on it sat china dishes of lobster, salad, fresh strawberries, scones, cakes and a pot of cream.

'Wow,' said Nigel. 'I don't think I've ever had a high tea like this before.'

'You just haven't lived, have you?' retorted Sue.

They were both still wearing their tennis whites and had come straight from their game. There were two chairs at the table, and a large bottle of wine stood in a silver cooler, with two glasses beside it.

'Isn't anyone else eating?' Nigel asked.

Sue shook her head. 'There's only the two of us in the house. Even maids insist on days off sometimes. Tom's working late, and the kids –'

'Are with your mother. I remember.'

She smiled at him – an innocent smile which Nigel knew was not innocent at all. He swallowed, looking at Sue and then at the food and wondering if he had the appetite for it all.

'Have you got any drink here?' Caines asked Alyson.

She sat at the table, her hands clasped together, her face blank with shock and grief. Slowly she shook her head.

Caines sat down opposite her, forcing her to look at him.

'How did it happen?' she asked.

'All I know at the moment is that his car went off the road at high speed and collided with something. It was very quick. I doubt if he even knew what was happening.'

Alyson digested this for a moment before suddenly appearing to come to a decision. She rose.

'I'm going to London. I want to go to the flat.'

'All right,' said Caines. 'I'll drive you.'

'I have to phone someone first. Thomas will need looking after.'

But she did not immediately go to the phone. She was staring at him as if she had just thought of something.

'Who phoned? And why did they phone *you*? What was Chris doing? What was he *really* doing?'

With a belly full of lobster and strawberries, Nigel lay sated on floor cushions beside the coffee table. Sue sat opposite him. The bottle of wine was empty, and Nigel felt blissfully content.

'The last time I had lobster,' he remarked, 'was at a restaurant in Brighton.'

'All on your own?' asked Sue.

'Oh, yes.'

'Poor Nigel.'

'They didn't give you much. It was all recipe and no meat, if you know what I mean. Do you eat like this all the time?'

'Only on special occasions.'

She was smiling at him, though Nigel wasn't sure exactly what the smile meant.

'I owed myself a treat,' she went on. 'It's good to relax and indulge yourself now and then, don't you think?'

Nigel nodded.

'I get tense very easily. It gets me in the neck. The muscles lock, and it hurts like hell. Of course, the best thing is a massage. Didn't you take that up at school?'

'What?'

'Massage.'

Sue had moved closer to him, and Nigel could smell the faint aroma of perfume and feminine sweat.

'I dabbled a bit,' he admitted.

Without warning, Sue stood up and peeled her tennis shirt off her back. Then she unhooked her bra and took it off. Nigel caught a glimpse of her breasts before she turned her back on him, then lay face-down across a cushion.

'Have a go at mine,' she said.

It was not an order Nigel could refuse, or resist. He laid his hands on her shoulder-blades, then ran his thumbs down either side of her spinal column. Her brown skin was warm, and as smooth as silk.

'Ahhh,' she said. 'That feels so good.'

'A hot bath would probably help,' he said feebly.

'There wouldn't be room, Nigel. I can only just stretch out on my own.'

Caines put down Chris Lucas's telephone and said to Alyson: 'That was Adam Bellman, a colleague of Chris's. He's coming over.'

Alyson had picked up a framed photograph of an elderly couple. 'I'll have to see his parents. They're both pretty feeble. He was very fond of them.'

Caines felt a numb sense of helplessness. 'Alyson, I want you to take off as much time as you need, OK? All I ask is that you call in each day and let me know how you are. Is it a deal?'

It was a moment before she nodded. 'Thank you. Are you leaving now?'

'Not unless you want to be alone.'

She shook her head. 'I'd rather you didn't go.'

'Some coffee, then? I could do with some.'

Caines went into the kitchen and rummaged around. He found a jar of Gold Blend and an unopened carton of milk in the fridge. It felt eerie to open the milk – milk which had been bought by Chris Lucas and which he would never drink. Caines had been unable to tell Alyson anything about Chris's work – he was as much in the dark as she.

They sat down opposite one another in armchairs, sipping their coffee. But Alyson's gaze roved around the room, as though she wanted to absorb every last impression of the place.

Presently she said, 'Thanks for driving me up here, Mr Caines.'

'Now hang on, Alyson. There's no way I'm going to be called "Mr Caines" by you on today of all days.'

She gave a thin smile. 'I'm not sure I could manage "Harry", frankly.'

'Try gritting your teeth.'

The doorbell rang, startling them both. Caines went to answer it and returned with Adam Bellman, a stocky man in his mid-thirties. Caines performed the introductions.

'Needless to say,' Bellman said to Alyson, 'I'm very sorry. Chris and I . . . well, we worked together for a long time.'

Alyson suddenly looked uncomfortable. 'What hospital was Chris taken to?'

'St Thomas's. It's not far from here.'

'I think I'd rather like to go now.'

'I'll fetch the car,' said Caines.

'No. I mean . . . I'd rather go alone. You don't mind?'

'Where will you stay tonight?'

'Here. Or maybe with some friends.' She smiled at his concern. 'I'll be fine now. Really. You'll lock up when you leave?'

Caines sensed that it was better not to argue. He nodded.

Alyson did not waste her time leaving. At the door she said, 'Thank you for coming over, Mr Bellman. Perhaps we could talk again some time.'

'Of course,' Bellman said.

She turned to Caines. 'And thank you again.' Then she

was gone.

Caines stood at the window, watching her drive away.

'She's standing up well,' Bellman remarked. 'But I would have thought she'd have wanted to know more about Chris – well, how it happened.'

'The funny thing is, she did – until you arrived. Then I think it all became too much for her. It's been a terrible day, and she's probably right to take things a little at a time. Coffee?'

Bellman nodded, and Caines went into the kitchen and made two further cups.

'Now,' said Caines when they were seated with their coffees, 'let's have a quick filling of the gaps. How exactly did he die?'

'You heard about the explosion last night?'

Caines shook his head.

'It was on the ten o'clock news. A travel agents was taken out, and properties either side of it. It's been all over the news.'

'I've been busy. What was it? A bomb?'

'A lorry packed with explosives. It was driven through the front window and left. Went up a few minutes later. We assumed it was one for the terrorist boys – nothing to do with us – but it just so happens that Chris was in the area at the time in his car. Another witness – a passerby – said that a couple of blokes scampered for a taxi after smashing the lorry through the window. Taxi must have been waiting for them, we reckon. Anyway, Chris takes off in pursuit and ends up – according to witnesses – wrapping his car around a stationary JCB.'

The coffee cup looked tiny in Bellman's big fist. He stared down at it, saying, 'It took almost two hours to cut him out. Not that there was any need to hurry.'

His smile was bleak and bitter.

'And that's it?' said Caines.

'For the moment.' Bellman sighed. 'We've spent weeks

on end watching the front doors of houses that no one ever visited. We talk to any number of people, most of them more of a hindrance than a help. Nine out of ten leads go nowhere at all. It's just plain slog – and then something like this happens.'

Caines didn't know what to say. They sipped their coffees in silence for a while.

'Had a look around, have you?' Bellman asked.

'No,' said Caines. 'No, I haven't.'

Bellman rose and began to rummage through cupboards and drawers.

'Chris may have been on to something hot,' he said. 'It's an outside chance, but he may have left something in writing.' He paused, then glanced at Caines. 'He never spoke to you about it?'

'Only in very general terms.'

'Cards close to the chest, old Chris. Always played it that way. His strength and his weakness. A lot of it's on your patch, you know.'

'Yes, I know.'

'And Miss Bentley? Think she could help?'

'No,' Caines said, quietly but firmly. 'Not yet.'

On his desk was a small photograph of Sue, taken just before they had married. Tom paused in his paperwork and stared at it. Things had been so good between them then – no arguments, no bitterness. He felt a longing for what had been lost and a sudden desire to recover it.

Reaching for the telephone, he began to dial his home number. Then he changed his mind and put the phone down: he wanted to *see* Sue. Rising, he took his coat off the back of the chair and walked out. The paperwork could wait.

He drove quickly home, wanting to hug her to him and promise her that everything would be all right from now on. But as he turned into the driveway, he noticed the blue

Morris Minor which was parked outside the house. It was Nigel's car.

The door itself was shut but not locked. Tom opened it quietly and walked into the hallway. A light was burning in the drawing room, and there was the murmur of voices. Suddenly Tom wanted to turn on his heels and walk out of the house, to drive far away. But he knew he would have to open the door. He hesitated for a moment, then stepped forward and turned the handle.

Sue was lying topless on a pile of scatter cushions with Nigel hovering over her, stroking her naked back. Nigel leapt up like a frightened rabbit on seeing him, but Sue sat up slowly and faced him without a trace of modesty or shame.

'Well,' she said with a faint, unhappy smile. 'Congratulations, darling. You've finally managed the unexpected.'

## *Chapter Twelve*

'Mr Caines wants to see us all in his office,' Calvin told Tom when he arrived at work the following morning.

'When?' Tom asked.

'Right now.'

Bruce and Nigel were already in Caines's office when they entered. Caines was seated at his desk, looking grim.

'I've got some bad news,' he said. 'Chris Lucas is dead.'

There was a stunned silence from Tom and the others. Caines told them everything he knew about Chris's death, adding, 'There's a big drugs thing going on, and it may be coming to roost on our patch. I've told Alyson to take as much time off as she needs, but I think she's going to want to be back at work soon. We've all got to do what we can to help her, but don't *overdo* it. She gave me the impression that she doesn't want us to make a big deal out of it.'

Tom and Calvin returned to their office.

'Poor Aly,' Calvin remarked.

'My God,' said Tom, 'what an unholy day!'

He was still shell-shocked by what had happened the night before. He took Sue's photograph from the desk and dropped it in the waste bin.

'Hey,' said Calvin. 'Wasn't that a picture of Sue?'

'No fooling you, is there? We're splitting up, Cal. She's already taken the kids to stay at her parents'. There's going to be a divorce.'

He and Sue had had a blazing row after Nigel had fled the house, and Sue was completely unrepentant, telling him he was a weakling and insisting he move out of *her* house.

Calvin was staring at him. 'I don't believe it,' he said.

'It's true. She wants me out of the house as soon as

possible. I don't own a thing there except my clothes.'

'She'll be back, Tom.'

'Not this time. It's the kids I'm worried about.'

Calvin was silent for a moment. Then he said, 'What exactly happened?'

Tom shrugged. 'We've been having row after row just lately. And last night I went home early and surprised her with someone else.'

'Someone else?'

'She had her shirt off, and he was giving her a massage. It was pretty tacky.'

'Do I know him? I'll wring his neck.'

'You know him all right, but he's hardly worth the exercise. She was just using him.'

'Who?'

'Our young friend Nigel.'

'Nigel??!! But he's only just out of short trousers.'

'She obviously likes them that way.'

'I'll have his guts for garters!'

'Not worth it, Cal. I'm sure she led him on.'

'Listen, Tom, if you need a place to stay, you only have to ask, OK?'

Tom gave a bleak smile. 'I appreciate that, Cal.'

The Langleys' drawing room was cluttered with children's toys and filled with the sound of infants' shrieking as James and Nichola wrestled with one another over the possession of a tricycle. In the middle of the mayhem, Jack and Helen Langley were trying to have a quiet cup of coffee.

'How long is this going to go on?' Jack said with a groan.

'Family life, darling,' replied Helen. 'Don't you remember?'

'Done my stint. Thought grandparents were supposed to have the fun without the bother.'

'It's only until Tom gets himself a place in town.'

'Park bench, I should think, on his salary. Why is the man

such a fool?'

'I don't think he's a fool exactly, darling. Just ridiculously honest.'

'We'd have made a good team, but that's water under the bridge now. Where's our darling daughter?'

'Still in bed, I assume. She's had a fairly traumatic experience.'

'I wouldn't have thought that young bloke was her type.'

'I don't think he is – she was just egging him on if I know Sue. I think she's got her eyes on a bigger fish.'

Jack peered at her. 'Who?'

'Isn't it obvious?'

'Not to me, it isn't.'

'Our friend Charles Thieron.'

'Never.'

'Raise the blinkers, Jack. We're always throwing them together.'

Jack swallowed a mouthful of tepid coffee. 'I'll tell you one thing – I'm not having a divorce in the family. I'll cut her off without a shilling.'

'Perhaps you should have made that clear.'

'I'm not having any muck sticking around the Langley name. Bad for business.'

'So why not tell our French friend to back off? He rings her all hours, asks her out. It can only lead one way.'

Jack shook his head. 'You tell him. Ours is a business partnership, and I'm not mixing it up with family affairs. You tell him.'

Helen Langley looked thoughtful. Presently she rose and went upstairs to her bedroom. Picking up the telephone, she punched out Charles Thieron's number. A butler answered.

'Can I speak to Monsieur Thieron, please,' she said. 'It's Helen Langley.'

She waited, and a few moments later heard Thieron say: 'Helen. How good to hear from you.'

'Hello, Charles. How are you?'

'I'm fine. And yourself?'

'Bearing up. Charles, I wonder if we could have a little talk some time soon.'

'Why of course. Dinner perhaps? I have the perfect restaurant in mind.'

Helen smiled. 'Sounds fine. When would you suggest?'

'Tonight? At eight?'

'You're quiet,' Nigel remarked to Calvin.

Calvin said nothing. He was rummaging through a pile of paperwork on one of the Long Room desks.

'What's the matter?' Nigel wanted to know.

'Tom's told me about what happened last night.'

'Oh, Cal, it was nothing, honestly. Sue had terrible tension in her neck and I was giving her a bit of a massage.'

'Tell us another one,' Calvin said sceptically. 'You're talking to an expert line-thrower, old son. Difference is I don't throw them to other people's ladies.'

'Neither do I.'

'Not much! You've been fawning around Sue like a Spanish waiter. We're not all blind and daft.'

'Well, I . . . I'm very fond of Sue. Always have been.'

'But she's not yours, matey, is she?'

'You don't have to rub it in.'

'Now she's not Tom's either.'

'What do you mean?'

'They've broken up, that's what I mean! And I'd like to give you a good hiding!'

Calvin stalked out, leaving Nigel aghast. He had never expected the incident to have such serious repercussions.

He picked up the telephone and dialled the Gibbons' house.

'This is a recorded message,' said the voice of Sue Gibbons, 'you can reach me at my parents' home.'

She gave the telephone number, and then the answerphone clicked off. Nigel, increasingly anxious, glanced up at the clock: it was almost lunchtime. He reached for his cap and hurried out of the building.

Climbing into his Morris Minor, he drove out of town to the Langley residence. Jack Langley was emerging from the house as Nigel got out of the car.

'Is Sue in, sir?' he asked.

'Yes she is,' said Jack. 'Aren't you the young fool that's caused all the trouble?'

'I've come to put things right.'

'Oh, well, I suppose that's something in your favour. She's out on the lawn.'

Nigel walked around to the back of the house. A bikini-clad Sue was lying on a sunbed, her eyes closed.

Nigel walked up to her. 'Sue?'

She opened her eyes. 'Oh, hello.'

'I've come to apologize.'

'What for?'

'I seem to have caused a bit of trouble.'

She gave a small shrug. 'Wasn't you, Nigel.'

'Well, I feel responsible.'

'You were only giving me a massage.'

'Yes. But it must have looked to Tom. . .'

'Oh, who cares? Tom'd suspect his own mother.'

Nigel felt awkward. 'Actually, I suppose it wasn't entirely innocent . . . was it?'

'Nigel! You amaze me.'

'If Tom hadn't come in . . . well, you're very attractive, Sue.'

'Thank you, kind sir.'

'And I've always . . . well, you know. Fancied you.'

'You're sweet.'

'But that doesn't mean I don't feel guilty about what happened.'

'Don't spoil it, Nigel.'

But Nigel was determined to say his piece. 'I'm sure you

didn't mean it, but you've placed me in a very difficult position. I have to work with Tom and the others –'

'What's it to do with the others?'

'Well, we're a pretty close-knit group.'

'Like the Boy Scouts.'

Sue's tone had abruptly changed from light-heartedness to scorn, and her smile had vanished. Nigel stared down at her.

'I seem to be wasting my time,' he said.

'Wasting somebody's,' she retorted coldly.

'I just thought . . . hoped . . . well, that we might be frank with one another.'

'There's nothing to be frank about, Nigel, is there? It was all quite innocent. Wasn't it?'

'If you say so.' He took a deep breath. 'But my apology still stands.'

'You'd better try it on Tom. He enjoys that sort of thing.'

Then she closed her eyes again, dismissing him as if he didn't exist.

The woman wore black corduroy trousers and a red weather-proofed jacket. She was in her thirties, with blonde hair and the most striking blue eyes that Calvin had ever seen.

'I have been waiting for two hours with my yellow flag flying,' she said to him in a Scandinavian accent. 'So now I come to give myself up.'

She removed her declaration forms from a waterproof sheet and laid them on the counter. Calvin did not normally do counter-duty, but the woman greatly intrigued him.

'You've goods to declare?' he asked her.

She indicated the forms. 'All filled in here correctly.'

Calvin glanced at them. 'You're a bit over the odds, aren't you?'

'I can pay for what I need.'

'You certainly need a lot of champagne.'

She smiled at him, revealing dazzlingly white teeth. 'I like to celebrate.'

Calvin smiled back. 'Don't we all.'

'Sometimes when I have a good run, or if it is just a good sunset, I celebrate, *ja*?'

'Come far?'

'From Stockholm. For me this is not so far.'

'What do you sail?'

'A Swan forty-five.'

Calvin whistled.

'You are also a sailor?' she asked him.

'In a small way. D'you race?'

'I used to. Then one day I was just cruising around in the Indian Ocean and I think – this is nice. Why race?'

'There are racing people and cruising people.'

'I am now a cruising person. But you are not making the addition.'

Calvin had been too busy looking into her big, blue eyes. He took a calculator off one of the desks.

The woman was watching him. 'Where is good to eat here?' she asked.

'Well,' said Calvin, 'there are one or two good seafood joints in the harbour.'

'Is it good helpings? In Sweden we have the smorgasbord – the cold table, you know? You can eat and eat and come back for more.' She laughed. 'I have a hearty appetite.'

Calvin grinned through his beard. 'You should try some plain English cooking.'

'English cooking is very plain, *ja*?'

'Depends who cooks it. And what wine you drink with it.'

'Wine is not English.'

'Not true. English wine is being taken very seriously indeed.'

'Really? I see you must educate me.'

'Be my pleasure.'

She studied him, her blue eyes sparkling. 'You must be my plain English cook. I invite myself. Unless you have wife or something?'

'Oh, no,' Calvin was quick to assure her.

'Good. Tonight then?'

The clock on the Long Room wall showed three-thirty. Nigel sighed; he was on duty till six, and the afternoon was dragging.

'Cheer up,' said Bruce, who was working at the desk opposite. 'You've got a face like a wet week. No use going round like a leper.'

Nigel shrugged morosely. 'I feel like one.'

Bruce studied him. 'Don't take it too hard, Nigel. If you want my opinion – which you probably don't – she isn't worth it.'

'If you'd said that yesterday, I'd have hit you. But now I've got to agree. How could I have been so wrong?'

'Love clouds the vision. Steams up the old specs.'

'It's no joking matter, Bruce.'

'I wasn't joking. Been to see her today, have you?'

Nigel nodded, surprised by Bruce's perspicacity. 'I wanted to apologize, but she gave me the brush off. She doesn't care about me – about anyone.'

'Maybe it's better to let things lie.'

'I keep going over it all in my mind.'

'Awful mistake. Wipe the slate clean, that's the job. Do you mind if I ask you a personal question?'

Nigel shook his head.

'You don't have to answer if you don't want to, but I was wondering – have you had many . . . I mean other women. Have there been any?'

Nigel looked him straight in the eye. 'I've loved Sue Langley since I was a schoolboy. There hasn't been room for anyone else.'

Bruce let out a sigh. 'That explains it.'

'What do you mean?'

'Why you couldn't see her as she is. Young love's pretty to watch, but it doesn't have much to do with the object of affection.'

Nigel looked puzzled. 'I'm not with you.'

'Well, at a certain age I think we're bound to fall for the nearest pretty object. And if we get a bit of encouragment there's no holding us – we invest that object with every desirable quality under the sun. But it's not real. We're making it up. And we make such a bloody good job of it that in the end we can't see the person at all.'

Nigel was surprised to hear all this from Bruce. Bruce never talked about his personal life, and he had assumed that he was a celibate academic who lived alone and had no experience of the opposite sex.

'I thought Calvin was the authority on romance in this office,' he said.

Bruce shook his head. 'Cal's had so much he's inoculated against it.'

'How about the lobster?' Charles Thieron suggested to Helen Langley.

'Fine,' she said. 'It's an aphrodisiac, isn't it?'

Thieron raised an eyebrow but said nothing.

A waiter hovered at their table, and Thieron turned to him. 'Two lobster, and then perhaps a fillet steak . . . rare? With a few potatoes sauteed?'

He had turned to Helen again. She nodded.

'And after that,' he went on, 'a sorbet or a salad?'

'You'll have to wheel me out of here, Charles.'

He returned her smile. 'Well, we shall decide later. And the wine . . . I think a Chablis with the lobster, don't you?'

'You're the expert.'

He turned back to the waiter. 'No. 22.' Then again to Helen: 'And with the steak – something fresh? A young

Cru Beaujolais? Chiroubles? Or do you prefer a nice dark claret.'

'It's all grape juice to me,' she said, straight-faced.

'You are jesting,' he said. And to the waiter: 'No. 11 and draw the cork at once, please.'

The waiter nodded curtly and withdrew. Thieron smiled at Helen across the table. 'Wines are like the places they come from. Each is different. When I drink a rough red from the Midi I already smell my home in Marseilles.'

The restaurant was one of the best – and most expensive – in the area. Helen was wearing a long black dress with a ruby necklace, while Thieron was attired in a dark suit with a burgundy tie which complemented her outfit perfectly. They made small talk until the lobsters arrived.

'I wanted to have a word with you about Sue,' Helen remarked presently. 'I'm rather worried about her.'

Thieron picked up her drift immediately. With an insouciant shrug, he said, 'Sue is attractive, but a child. I play with like a puppy. This is amusing but *pas sérieux*.'

'I'd like you to cool it.'

He spread his hands in ready acceptance. 'It is cool. You only have to say it. *Voilà*, like a magician.'

'Thank you, Charles. I knew you'd understand.'

He was studying her, a faint smile on his lips. 'I play with the daughter because perhaps the mother she is out of reach. What man would go for the copy if he could have the real thing?'

Helen laughed. 'Charles, you have the perfect line in patter.'

'I am serious.'

She stared back at him. 'I do believe you are. And I'm flattered. But also hungry. Shall we eat?'

They attended to their meal. The food was superb, as was the wine which Thieron had chosen. Helen was aware that his eyes were on her throughout, and she enjoyed the attention. When they talked she was at turns provocative and coy. It was a game she had played often and successfully in the past; it was a game she loved.

Thieron, she knew, was smitten by the challenge she was offering him. She had taken a taxi to the restaurant, but when the meal was over she did not decline his offer to drive her home in his Mercedes.

It was a clear, calm night, the stars brilliant in the dark sky. Thieron drove them down a quiet lane, then suddenly pulled up. He turned and reached for her, but at the last moment she drew back.

He regarded her in the orange glow of a streetlamp. She could see the desire in his eyes.

'You are right,' he said. 'In the motor car is not very romantic for mature people. We will go home to my place.'

She shook her head. 'My place, Charles.'

'Your place?'

'I mean just take me home, please.'

'I don't understand.'

'I'm sorry, Charles.'

Thieron stared at her in silence for a moment. Then he shrugged and put the car into gear.

'So what do you think of the wine?' Calvin asked his companion.

'Good,' she said. 'A hock?'

'An English reisling from the Sussex downs, Annie.'

Annie Soldstrom laughed and said, 'I learn something every day.' She peered around the cottage. 'And you live here all alone?'

'Like a hermit,' said Calvin, po-faced.

She grinned at him with patent disbelief. They were sitting opposite one another at a candle-lit table and had just finished off a meal of roast beef and Yorkshire pudding, fresh peas and new potatoes which Calvin had cooked himself.

'The food was very good,' Annie said. 'You are an excellent cook, and I will not say bad things about the English cuisine again.'

'And now,' said Calvin, 'some brandies, yes?'

She nodded enthusiastically.

He poured the brandies, and they sat down on a sofa in front of the blazing log fire. It wasn't cold, but the fire provided an intimate atmosphere. Annie sat close to Calvin, and he could hardly stop looking at her. Their conversation quickly turned to sailing.

'I used to crew yachts out of Bridgetown,' he told her. 'The Caribbean is nice. Plenty of breeze. But best of all is the Pacific. So vast. You can go for days without seeing any sail but your own.'

'Sounds a bit lonely.'

She shook her head. 'When you enjoy to be alone is when you grow up as a sailor.'

'In that case, I'm probably doomed to adolescence. More brandy?'

'Perhaps one more. Then bed, *ja*?'

Calvin stared at her with open admiration. He gave an eager, broken-backed nod.

# *Chapter Thirteen*

The doorbell rang. Harry Caines stumbled from bed and donned his dressing gown before padding over to the door and opening it. It was Alyson.

'Sorry to call so early,' she said as he ushered her inside. 'Couldn't sleep.'

'That's OK. Coffee?'

'Please. I seem to be living on it at the moment.'

Caines put the kettle on and spooned coffee into two mugs.

'I wanted to ask you a favour,' Alyson said hesitantly.

'Ask away,' he told her.

'Well, several favours, actually.'

'Fine.'

'The funeral – there's an awful lot of arranging to do –'

'No problem. I was going to offer to do it anyway.'

'Thanks. They seem to make dying more complicated these days.'

'I'll see to it.'

'And then there's what to do with his flat.'

'Did he own it?'

'Long lease.'

'Is it any use to you or your parents?'

She shook her head.

'Then we'll put it in the hands of one or two estate agents. Should sell quickly enough. Who gets the money?'

'Oh, his parents, I hope. I'd want them to.'

'Shouldn't be much difficulty about that. Did he have a solicitor?'

'Not a regular one, I don't think.'

'Doesn't matter. We'll use mine.'

Alyson sighed irritably. 'I really despise myself playing the helpless female.'

'Don't,' Caines told her. 'Male or female has nothing to do with it. The man's just as helpless in this situation, believe me.'

She stared at him, then nodded.

Caines poured hot water into the two coffee mugs.

'There's one more thing,' said Alyson. 'It's a bit of an imposition, but I thought I'd ask.'

'Go on,' said Caines.

'Some of the better furniture. We were planning to sell it. The parents won't want it, and I've no room at the cottage. I was wondering. . .'

'You're offering to set me up in style?'

'Would you mind? It's good quality stuff.'

'I'd hate to be the one to profit from disaster.'

'It's an ill wind, Harry. Chris would have approved. He liked you a lot, and respected you. And I respect you.'

Her eyes were filling up.

'All right,' said Caines. 'It's a deal.' He had sold all his belongings after the death of his wife and children in order to buy the 'Lotus'.

They sat down and drank their coffees.

Alyson said, 'Do you know any more about what happened to Chris?'

'Adam Bellman's the man you have to speak to. He's told me only as much as he wants. You know how ID operate.'

'Will they continue working out of this area?'

'I imagine they'll have no option.'

She stared out the window. 'I was thinking – there are vacancies in ID, aren't there?'

Caines guessed what was coming. 'Yes,' he said.

'If I applied – you'd support me?'

He waited until she was looking at him. 'No. At the moment you wouldn't be the best of candidates. Please don't try to get involved in the Chris business.'

She was silent, though he could see the anger in her face.

'If you think that's hard,' he added, 'it's meant to be.'

'My man's been killed,' Alyson said vehemently. 'I loved him and I'll do anything to find the bastards who ran him down. Don't try to stop me.'

'Everyone wants to find them, Alyson – me as much as anyone else. But what you need now is a little bit of time to come to terms with what's happened. Then try and think about it calmly. In the long run you'll serve Chris's memory far better that way, I promise you.'

Caines was speaking from the heart, and Alyson knew this. She looked a little shamefaced. 'I'm sorry, Harry. I didn't mean to fly off the handle.'

'No need to apologize – I know what it's like. Try to absorb yourself in the other things in your life. Like Thomas, for example.'

'I'm not neglecting him. More than ever I want to get through to Wembley – for Chris and for myself.'

The boot of the Cavalier was filled with luggage. Helen Langley closed it while a surprised Sue looked on.

'But why so sudden?' she asked her mother.

'Whim, darling. And anyway it won't do any harm to open up the villa. Give it a good airing.'

'You said nothing yesterday.'

'Well, that's what whims are, aren't they, Sue? They come on you suddenly and you have to give in.'

Sue peered at her. 'Are you trying to tell me something?'

'I don't think there's much I can tell you about whims.'

'What did Jack say?'

'"Marbella? Do you good. Wish I could come."'

'Seems funny to me.'

'No doubt. Other people's whims often do.'

'You're getting at me, aren't you?'

'No, darling. I'm going for a much-needed holiday.'

* * *

Jack Langley pulled his Daimler up outside the Gibbons house. He went to the front door and was about to ring the bell. Changing his mind, he produced a key from his pocket and opened the door.

The house was quiet, and Jack climbed the stairs to the bedrooms. Tom was shaving in front of the bathroom mirror, and he gave a start as Jack walked into the doorway.

'How did you get in?' Tom asked.

'Sue's keys. I wanted to have a word with you.'

'I've got to get to work.'

'Things are moving along, Tom. Sue's seeing her uncle the solicitor today. Getting the divorce moving.'

Tom shrugged and dabbed the shaving foam from his face with a towel.

'There's still time,' Jack said.

'For what?'

'To patch things up. All you have to do is take the job.'

'No.'

'Is that your final answer?'

'Completely.'

Jack lounged in the doorway while Tom searched for a fresh shirt.

'You know,' he remarked, 'Sue listens to me.'

'And more or less to everyone else. But she always ends up doing exactly what she wants.'

'You'll have nothing left, boy.'

'Depends on how you view it.'

'House and car. They're in my name.'

'The old street-trader.'

'Getting what I want – for my daughter.'

Tom went to his jacket and produced a set of keys. He tossed them on the bed. 'Those are the car keys. Sue has the second set. I'll be out of here by the weekend, and I'd like you to get out now.'

'Bluff, Tom.'

'Called.'

'And the kids? You'll not get them. Not a prayer.'

The breakfast tray held hot croissants, butter, honey and a pot of fresh-ground coffee. Annie Soldstrom was dozing, but her eyes opened as Calvin set the tray down on the bedside table.

'Breakfast is served, madame,' he said with a smile.

She yawned, stretched. Calvin perched himself on the end of the bed, peering down at her. She had been staying with him for the past few days, and Calvin knew he was hooked.

'Thought I'd take you out to dinner tonight,' he said. 'The yacht club.'

She was studying the breakfast tray. 'Why there?'

'We're both sailors, aren't we? Besides the food's good.' He tweaked one of her toes. 'Though not as good as you.'

Charles Thieron stood inside his bird house with Sayed el Mahkted, a Harrow-educated prince of an Arabian royal family. Falcons had long been a passion of both Thieron and Mahkted, and they had just been watching one of Thieron's four Peregrines take a rabbit on the wild hillside above Thieron's mansion. Now the bird was back in its pen, and Thieron and Mahkted were discussing business.

'My offer stands,' Mahkted told Thieron. 'You can have the next consignment in exchange for the four birds, or for just the Gyr. That's worth £80,000, Charles.'

Thieron shook his head. 'You inflate the market, Sammy – bad for business. But no deal. When the Gyr arrives, it stays with me. And the Peregrines, too.'

Mahkted gave a crafty look. 'I can cut off your merchandise, Charles.'

'What will you do for money then, my friend? Hope that your family will take you under its wing again?'

Mahkted looked disgruntled. His father had disinherited

him several years ago, and there was no prospect of a reconciliation between them.

'It was a joke about stopping the cannabis, Charles. The ship is already on its way.'

'Arriving?'

'Depends on Biscay. They'll radio.'

'Good. Breakfast now? And go easy on those girls, Sammy. You haven't got them back to the Gulf yet.'

They went through a door which led down a corridor to the main part of Thieron's mansion. Two girls in their late teens were laying the breakfast table. They were beautiful and dressed only in cotton wraps. The telephone was ringing in the adjoining room, and Thieron went to answer it as Mahkted put his arms around both the girls' waists.

The call was from one of Thieron's men in Portugal. The Gyrfalcon had been delivered and was awaiting pick-up in Lisbon.

'Excellent,' Thieron said. 'I will come immediately.'

He hung up, then punched out Jack Langley's number. He was due to have a business lunch with Langley, but the white falcon had to take precedence.

He heard the phone being picked up and a female voice said, 'Hello?'

Thieron smiled into the receiver. 'Ah, Sue. It is Charles. I wanted Jack.'

'Good morning, Charles. I'm afraid Jack's out.'

'Then would you please tell him that alas I must cancel our lunch date today. Something urgent has come up.'

'He *will* be disappointed.'

'I shall make it up to him, I assure you.' Thieron paused, considering. 'Perhaps you would like a trip to Lisbon?'

'Lisbon? When?'

'Today Immediately. Quickly there and back. My cruiser, then a plane. One day.'

'It's rather short notice, Charles.'

'Ah, well. Some other time, perhaps.'

'I didn't say I wouldn't come. When do you want me to be ready?'

'In one hour?'

'Fine. I'll leave a message for Jack.'

The telephone on Nigel's desk rang. He picked it up and listened for a moment before putting his hand over the mouthpiece.

'Someone's winding us up,' he said to Brucc, who was seated opposite. 'Says it's the Home Office – a Minister. For you.'

Bruce did not look surprised. He took the receiver from Nigel.

'Tomlin?' he said. 'Yes, I'll wait. . . Oh, hello, Ronald. . . I'm fine. And you? . . . Thank you. . . They publish in six months. . . No, I'm too busy to come to London at the moment. . . Yes, nice of you to ring. Bye.'

Bruce put the phone down. Nigel could not hide his curiosity.

'All right,' said Bruce, 'that was my brother, Ronald Tomlin, MP. My other brother's famous, too, in the City. And my father's elderly and eminent. I also have a wife who lives in Switzerland. Anything else you want to know?'

Nigel was astounded. 'A wife?'

'Why should you find that so surprising?'

Nigel looked confused. 'But you don't live together, do you?'

'She's a geologist. Travels a lot on oil exploration projects. We see one another when we can.'

Tom Gibbons had appeared in the doorway, a suitcase in each hand.

'Did you hear that?' Nigel asked him.

'I heard it,' Tom said without looking at him. 'You're a dark horse, Bruce.'

The words were said without enthusiasm: Tom looked downcast. He turned and went next door to his own office.

Calvin, seeing his suitcases, said, 'You've moved out?'

Tom nodded, then told him about Jack Langley's visit that morning.

'Naturally he saw it all as debit and loss,' he told Calvin. 'Anyway, I'd like to take up your offer.'

'Offer?'

'Of bed and board.'

Calvin looked rueful. 'You haven't been listening to me the past few days, Tom. I've got Annie living with me.'

'Annie?'

'I did try to tell you about her. She's someone special. I'm smitten, old boy – I admit it.'

When Tom said nothing, Calvin went on: 'I'm sorry, Tom. I didn't plan it.'

Tom shook his head. 'It's all right. Rather ironic, actually. Me suddenly being free, and you seeing stars.'

'Never thought it would happen to me. I really wish I could help.'

'Don't worry, I'll find somewhere else. I suppose I'd better let Caines know what's happened.'

Determined to get it over with, Tom went directly to Caines's office.

'I thought you ought to know,' he said. 'I've left home.'

'Oh,' said Caines.

'More like it's being repossessed. Father-in-law.'

'I'm very sorry, Tom.'

Tom shrugged. 'In some ways I feel relieved – if it wasn't for the kids. Anyway, I wanted you to know, for the records. I'll be looking for a place –'

'I've got a spare room, Tom.'

'What?'

'If it wouldn't be too big a fall from grace, you're welcome to it.'

Tom stared at him. 'I don't know what to say. Except thank you.'

'Move in whenever you like.'

He offered Tom the keys of the flat.

'Can I take my cases over now?'

'Certainly.' Caines gave a faint smile. 'You can also wash up the breakfast things.'

Arriving home, Jack Langley found Thieron waiting outside his house.

'Caught me on the hop, Charles,' he said.

'It's not business, Jack. I'm picking up Sue. Didn't she say?'

'Just got back from the airport. Helen decided that she needed a bit of sun, so she's off to Marbella. You two had a pleasant evening?'

'Very pleasant,' Thieron said, his expression betraying nothing. 'Helen did not mention Marbella.'

'Typical. Very unsettled, my two ladies at the moment. You know about the Tom business?'

'Yes.'

'So I'm now thinking of putting my entire operation on offer. Interested?'

'Everything?'

'The lot. Too rich for you?'

'I'm very interested, Jack. But I'm afraid we'll have to postpone our lunch. We'll talk when we get back.'

'I didn't know you were going anywhere.'

'A day's excursion to Portugal. I'm taking Sue.'

Jack frowned. 'Charles, I know she's her own woman and all that –'

'Just a little adventure.'

Before Jack could air his misgivings further, Sue herself appeared, dressed in a cream jacket and white culottes. She greeted them both with kisses.

'So what's this day-trip in aid of?' Jack asked.

'In absolute confidence,' said Thieron, 'I am picking up a Gyrfalcon which is waiting for me in Lisbon.'

Jack knew a thing or two about falcons. 'I thought Gyrs were cold climate birds.'

'Indeed. And I have been promised an almost white bird from Greenland. Very rare.'

'So what's it doing in Lisbon?'

'It has made a long journey by unseen aeroplanes to New York. Then by diplomatic baggage to Lisbon. And now it's almost mine.'

So the bird was illegal. Jack scrutinized Thieron. 'Any danger in this, Charles?'

'Absolutely none, I assure you.'

Sue looked excited by the prospect of the trip.

'Anything you want from Lisbon?' she asked her father.

Through the window, evening was falling over Wrelling harbour. Harry Caines cracked open two cans of lager as Tom entered from the spare bedroom.

'Not too cramped in there?' Caines asked.

'No,' said Tom. 'And thanks again. I'll find somewhere as soon –'

'There's no rush, Tom.'

Tom accepted the proffered lager and sat down. He peered around the flat.

'This takes me back,' he remarked.

'Bachelor days?'

'Oh, don't get me wrong. There's a lot to be said for it.'

'The comforts are courtesy of Alyson. She let me have some of the furniture.'

'How do you think she's coping?'

'She'll get by. I've been dropping in on her most evenings, and she's bearing up. Strong lady.'

'That's true,' Tom agreed. 'I only wish Sue had half her moral fibre.'

Caines peered at him. 'Are you hoping to patch things up?'

'Nothing would change if I did. Jack would still want me in harness – he'd still believe that money buys everything.'

'And Sue?'

'Even if she decided to grow up, I probably wouldn't like the adult any more than the child. But I'm determined to get the kids.'

'Will you stay for a meal?' Alyson asked Bruce and Nigel.

'No, really,' said Bruce. 'We just dropped by to see you.'

'Bruce's idea,' said Nigel, 'and a good one, too. He's a surprising man, is Bruce. Did you know he was married?'

Bruce gave a long-suffering sigh before telling Alyson about his wife. They had met at a seminar which his father, then a professor of geology at London University, had given ten years ago. He had married Lotte soon afterwards, though they had never lived together for any great length of time.

'We meet twice a year at Lotte's home in Lausanne,' Bruce told Alyson. 'It suits us both.'

To Nigel, the arrangement was strange, but Alyson, better versed in the ways of the world, was more understanding. Both Bruce and Lotte were academics and very committed to their respective careers and hobbies; Alyson knew that for some people romance was a secondary rather than primary aspect of their lives.

'How's Thomas?' Nigel asked. He had only recently discovered that Thomas was in fact a horse.

'He's fine,' Alyson said. 'Tomorrow's the County Show. If I get through, it's Wembley next.'

'You're still going to ride?'

'I have to carry on, Nigel. Riding Thomas is helping me stay sane. And Chris would have expected me to.'

There was silence for a moment.

'Need any help with him?' Nigel asked.

'Oh, yes. Fetching and carrying. Mucking out. Picking his feet.'

'Pardon?'

'Of straw and manure.'

'Sounds gruesome.'

She smiled. 'I have some chums here and there who'll help out. But thanks for the offer. Now, shall we get some grub organized?'

The meal had been excellent, and Calvin had drunk his fill of good burgundy. He sat in the bar with Annie, staring round the room from time to time.

'Expecting someone?' Annie asked. And with a hint of mischief: 'Another woman, perhaps?'

'No, no. Just seeing if I know anyone.'

'Cal, it is getting late. We go home now, yes?'

Calvin glanced at his watch; it was approaching midnight. He had been reluctant to leave the Yacht Club because he had spotted the white Mercedes which belonged to Charles Thieron in the car park as they were arriving. But there had been no sign of the Frenchman all evening.

'Cal,' Annie said with just a hint of impatience, 'I am tired. Please, let us go.'

Calvin gave in. 'All right.'

They walked outside. It was a warm, clear night with a crescent moon. Suddenly Calvin spotted a cruiser which he recognized. He stopped in his tracks.

'What is it?' Annie asked.

'That cruiser. It's just come in. Thieron's.'

'Who is this?'

'Charles Thieron. A Frenchman who hangs around here. He's into something big and illegal. I've been keeping an eye on him.'

'Cal,' Annie said, a note of exasperation in her voice, 'I want to go home now.'

Suddenly Calvin saw Thieron walk off the launch towards his car. Immediately behind him came Sue Gibbons. Thieron was carrying a large box with holes in its side. Calvin immediately recognized it as a bird-box, and his suspicions were fully aroused. Neither Thieron nor Sue had noticed them.

'He's got a bird,' Calvin said. 'I bet he's sneaking it in.'

'You are off duty. We go home.'

Annie tried to drag him towards their car, but Calvin resisted.

'I've got to find out what it is.'

He made to move forward, but Annie stepped in front of him. She looked angry.

'Calvin,' she said, 'I am tired and not pleased. You have paid me no attention since we eat. You take me home now, or I will get a taxi. And I will not be at your cottage when you get back.'

# *Chapter Fourteen*

Crouched on the mountainside with a pair of binoculars in his hands, Calvin waited. It was early morning, and he had risen at six o'clock, leaving Annie profoundly asleep, before driving out to the Thieron mansion. By agreeing to take Annie home from the Yacht Club he had let Thieron slip out of his clutches; but instinct told him that he might get another chance if he was patient.

Half an hour passed. Then an hour. Bundled up in his overcoat, Calvin was nevertheless chilly in the brisk morning air. Then suddenly he saw a trio of figures emerge from the house. The first was unmistakably Thieron, the second Sue Gibbons, the third a man he didn't recognize but who looked Middle-Eastern. But most important of all was the bird which Thieron had tethered to his arm – a white falcon.

After a moment, Thieron released the bird. Calvin grinned and reached for the Pentax which was slung over his shoulder.

An hour and a half later, he was knocking on the door of Harry Caines's office, the newly developed prints still wet in his hands.

'Come,' said Caines.

Calvin walked in. 'I've got him, sir! Thieron!'

With breathless haste, Calvin told Caines what had happened. Then he spread the prints out on the desk.

Caines studied them, then said, 'They're pretty good on sky, Calvin, but there's nothing conclusive here. Everything's so blurred you could take this bird for a seagull.'

'Slight problem with the focus,' Calvin had to agree. 'But it was a falcon of some sort.'

Caines pondered, then picked up the internal telephone.

'Bruce?' he said into it, 'could you bring in those posters of endangered bird species.'

A few minutes later Bruce appeared with the posters.

'Calvin reckons he's seen Thieron with a falcon,' Caines said.

'He keeps Peregrines, sir,' Bruce told him. 'Four, I gather. All legal and decent.'

'This was a white bird,' Calvin said.

'Indeed?' Bruce's curiosity was immediately aroused. He studied one of the posters, then pointed. 'Could it have been that?'

Calvin looked at the indicated bird. 'Yes, I'm sure that was it.'

'Well, well,' said Bruce. 'A Gyrfalcon, and a very rare variety. Pricey bird.'

'Are you certain it wasn't ringed?' Caines asked Calvin.

'As good as. In any case, why was Thieron sneaking it off his cruiser in a box by night if it was legal?'

'You can't be sure the Gyrfalcon was inside the box,' Caines reminded him.

Calvin merely shrugged.

Bruce said, 'Shall I get on to the DOE in Bristol, sir? They'd have a record of all registered birds.'

'Do that,' said Caines.

Bruce went out.

'I thought it was your day off,' Caines said to Calvin.

Calvin grinned. 'New hobby, sir. Ornithology.'

Five minutes later, Bruce returned. 'I got through to a Mr Franklin, sir – he's the Chief Wildlife Inspector at Bristol. Mr Thieron has four Peregrines listed, but no Gyrfalcon. The inspector's driving down here as soon as possible, but he's still on the line. He wants to speak to you first.'

Caines picked up the telephone.

By the time Franklin arrived in Wrelling, Caines and

Calvin had made a trip out to the vicinity of Thieron's mansion to plot all the exit routes from the building so that they could be covered. Franklin, a dark-haired man in his forties, asked how Calvin had found out about the Gyrfalcon.

'Thieron's interested me for some time,' Calvin told him.

Franklin glanced at Caines. 'Is this likely to muddy your waters?'

'I shouldn't think so,' Caines said.

'Right. I've got five of my people to cover the grounds. But the approach will be softly, softly. Don't want any birds to fly. Myself and you, Calvin – we'll do the knocking on the door.'

Caines said, 'Any objections to me coming along?'

Calvin gave a rueful smile. 'I'm not completely trusted hereabouts.'

'Wrong, Cal,' Caines told him. 'I want to see Thieron's reactions.'

'All right,' said Franklin. 'But I think we ought to get a move on. That Gyr might be carrying Newcastle disease.'

'What's that?' asked Calvin.

'Fowl pest. The falcon hasn't been quarantined. Birds of prey are fed with day-old male chicks. The owner of an infected falcon calls at the hatchery and – *voilà* – in six weeks half the chicken population could be wiped out.'

Standing on the landing, Sue Gibbons watched Thieron and Sammy Mahkted in relaxed conversation below. She felt neglected and bored. Somewhere upstairs a door opened, and presently a woman of Sue's own age came down the stairs towards her.

'You coming with us?' she asked Sue.

'Where?'

'On the plane. To the Gulf.'

'Not as far as I know. What plane?'

The woman took a moment to answer. 'Sammy's. Money's great. Shoot up whenever you like.'

Her eyes were bright and dark. She was high, Sue realized.

'What do you do?' Sue asked her.

The woman shrugged. 'Entertain – or whatever they want.'

Then she wandered unsteadily off down the corridor.

Suddenly Sue heard a car drawing up outside. Below, Thieron had gone to the window.

'Sammy,' he said, 'we have some unexpected guests. I think it's best if you were not seen.'

Sammy immediately slipped away. There was a knocking on the door.

'Mr Caines,' said Thieron as he opened it. 'Do come in.'

'Thank you, Mr Thieron.'

'Of course you know the house. The twinning reception, wasn't it?'

'That's right, Mr Thieron.'

'And now?'

Caines introduced Franklin and Calvin. 'Mr Franklin is a wildlife inspector from the Department of the Environment in Bristol. We understand that you keep Peregrines here, Mr Thieron.'

'That is correct. Four birds, all registered.'

'And no others?'

'None,' Thieron said with perfect aplomb.

'We'd like to see the falcons,' Franklin said.

'Why, of course,' Thieron replied.

He ushered them down the corridor which led to the bird house. While they inspected the Peregrines, Thieron fetched his licence. Franklin checked the details against his computer print-out.

'Seems to be in order,' he said finally.

Thieron smiled. 'And so very well cared for, aren't they? You surprise me. Three of you for such a visit.'

'Falcons face extinction, Mr Thieron,' Franklin told him. 'We have to be careful they don't get into the wrong hands.

You have no other birds, you said?'

'None that are relevant to your concerns.'

Caines was peering around the bird house. There was a further door in the opposite wall.

'And through there?' he asked.

Thieron forced a smile. 'Why such persistence, Mr Caines?'

'I like to be thorough. Through there?'

'Nothing, I assure you.'

Suddenly Sue Gibbons entered from the house.

'What's going on?' she asked. 'Hello, Calvin. Hello, Mr Caines.'

Caines nodded, then said, 'I think it would be better if you excused us, Mrs Gibbons.'

'Why?'

'We won't keep Mr Thieron any longer than necessary. Perhaps you'd like to wait outside?'

Sue did not like being treated as an unwelcome intruder; she did not like being excluded. She turned to Thieron. 'Charles?'

'Do as he says, Sue.'

'Oh well,' she said. 'I know how boring Customs work is.' Then she flounced out.

The moment she was gone, Franklin said, 'Tell me about this feather, Mr Thieron.'

Unnoticed by the others, Franklin had picked up a mottled white feather from the floor of the bird house.

Thieron shrugged. 'It's a feather.'

'Doesn't match any of your birds.'

Thieron stared at him. 'You are the expert.'

'Then I'll offer an opinion. I think it's a Gyrfalcon feather, Mr Thieron. Would you open that door, please?'

Thieron forced a smile, but Caines could see the fury beneath it. Taking a key from his pocket, he unlocked the door. In the small room beyond, the Gyrfalcon was tethered to a perch.

'Do you have a licence for this falcon?' Franklin asked Thieron.

'No.'

'An export permit from the country of origin?'

'No.'

'Then we have to detain this bird. And your other falcons will be seized.'

Sue Gibbons was waiting angrily in the driveway when Caines and the others emerged with the Gyrfalcon in a cage which Franklin had brought with him.

'I don't like being told what to do, Mr Caines,' she began.

'Don't be daft, Sue,' said Calvin.

'Keep out of this, Cal. I'm talking to your boss.'

'Mrs Gibbons,' said Caines, 'this may not be the most appropriate place for you at the moment.'

'Because of Tom? He's nothing to do with me any more.'

'He's still your husband, Mrs Gibbons. And he's still a Customs officer.'

Franklin, who was loading the Gyrfalcon into the back of his grey Volvo estate, looked up at this. But Sue was already stalking towards her car.

'What's Thieron likely to face?' Caines asked Franklin.

'I'll be throwing the book at him, which is what he deserves. He'll probably get about a twenty thousand pound fine. And the loss of his birds.'

Calvin grinned through his beard. 'How tragic.'

'And a five year ban on keeping birds of prey.'

'Well, well,' said Caines. 'What an unhappy Frenchman we'll have on our hands.'

But Thieron was furious rather than unhappy. Inside the house, he was already on the internal telephone to two of his men who were upstairs.

'A grey Volvo estate is leaving by the main entrance,' he told them. 'They have the Gyr. I want you to follow them until they drop the bird. Let me know immediately.'

* * *

Slumped in an armchair with a stiff gin and tonic in her hand, Sue Gibbons regarded her father. She was ruffled, edgy.

'Did you know Charles had women about that house?' she asked.

'Yes,' said Jack Langley.

'Who are they?'

He shrugged. 'Didn't ask.'

'It was creepy. One of them was as high as a kite.'

'So be warned.'

'Oh, not you, too.'

Jack lit a cigar. 'You'd better tell me what happened.'

'Caines turned up – about one of Charles's falcons.'

'Oh? Anything to do with the Lisbon trip?'

'Yes. The white bird. They took it away.'

'Well, well. Charles caught napping, was he?'

'You're doing some deal with him, aren't you?'

'Larger than I intended since Tom turned me down. I'm unloading all my business.'

There was silence for a moment. Sue looked sheepish. 'You know that Charles and I . . . well, we've had trips together.'

Jack nodded solemnly.

'Do you think . . . well, what *do* you think?'

'Age gaps – generation gaps – have their disadvantages.'

'It's worked with you and Helen.'

'Hasn't been a smooth ride all the way, Sue. Sometimes plain old steady is best. I'm going to give you some advice – don't mess around with Thieron.'

Sue was unconvinced. 'I'll see what Mummy says. I'll ring her.'

'I mean it,' Jack said adamantly. 'He'll only bring you grief. Listen to me, Sue. Don't mess around with him.'

* * *

'I believe you now,' Caines said to Calvin as they sat together in his office. 'Thieron could repay a bit of attention. What do you think Sue Gibbons was doing there?'

Calvin shrugged. 'Having her own way, as usual. So what do you make of Thieron, sir?'

'Beneath that urbane façade, I think he's a very ruthless man. There's certainly much more to him than meets the eye.'

Calvin stroked his beard. 'I've got a feeling he's involved in this cannabis thing.'

'What makes you say that?'

'He's building one hell of a front, sir. Why get involved with Jack Langley? Peanuts for Thieron, judging by his business interests on the continent. He's been nosing around this and that since he arrived – a smiling, respectable figure in the background. He's a man with an eye for the main chance, and his overseas connections put him in the ideal position to smuggle drugs into the country.'

'You may be right,' said Caines, 'but we haven't got anything conclusive on him as yet. Let's be cautious. Don't mention to Tom that Sue was at Thieron's house. And for God's sake don't mention drugs and Thieron to Alyson. She's a very angry lady. By the way – have you heard?'

'What?'

'Alyson phoned in just before lunch while we were out. She and Thomas have got through to Wembley.'

The house stood isolated in the countryside under cover of darkness. It was surrounded by outbuildings housing valuable birds and animals which had been confiscated by DOE inspectors.

The van turned quietly into the approach road, and two men got out. Several hours earlier they had followed Franklin's Volvo to the house and had seen the Gyrfalcon delivered to the elderly man who ran the wildlife sanctuary. Now they had come to reclaim the bird.

Both men were dressed in black, and both carried heavy clubs. As they approached the house, a dog began to bark. Out of the darkness, an Alsatian came surging towards them. But both men were ready, clubbing the dog swiftly and heavily into unconsciousness.

They walked up to the door and knocked on it.

'Who's there?' said a voice from inside.

'We have an injured barn owl,' said one of the men. 'Can you help?'

As the door was opened from within, both men raised their clubs.

'Have you lodged your flight plan?' Charles Thieron asked Sammy Mahkted early the following morning.

'Four days ago,' he replied. 'I'd better get moving.'

'When will your ship be off the Lizard?'

'Two days.'

'Good. I'm ready, and so's the market.'

The two men walked out of the house and stood on the driveway.

'I'm so glad you're taking the bird,' Thieron said. 'It's worth the price of the consignment. Customs will have to be satisfied with my Peregrines. But I must be more careful in future. That Sue – she's bad luck.'

'As long as our consignment hasn't been compromised. We must pay our respects to seven tonnes of Lebanese Gold.'

'How true. The bird will be waiting for you at the airport. And the girls.'

Mahkted smiled broadly. 'I can hardly wait.'

Caines and Tom were having an early breakfast at the flat when the telephone rang. It was Calvin, phoning from the Custom House.

Caines took his message, looking grim.

'What's up?' asked Tom.

'The falcon we took from Thieron yesterday. It's been nicked. A couple of thugs coshed the chap who runs the safe house last night. He's in hospital with concussion and the Gyrfalcon's vanished.'

'Damn,' said Tom. 'Thieron must be behind it.'

'Pretty obvious, I'd say. The question is: what's he likely to do with the bird?'

'It won't be at his house. He's sure to know the police will be watching him.'

'I agree. But falcons aren't the easiest things to hide. I think he'll be wanting to get it out of the country as soon as possible.'

'His cruiser?'

'Too obvious. And Calvin has sent Alyson over to the marina to keep an eye on things there.'

'She's back on duty?'

Caines nodded. He was thinking furiously. Going to the telephone, he dialled Westholme Airport and asked if there were any private flight departures that day.

'Yes, sir,' said the man at the other end of the line. 'One this morning – a Sayed el Mahkted.'

Caines took down the relevant details, then hung up. To Tom he said, 'We've got a Sayed el Mahkted flying out this morning.'

'Sounds like an Arab. Didn't Calvin mention something about a Middle-Eastern type being with Thieron when he was photographing the falcon?'

Caines nodded; Calvin had also been discreet enough not to mention that Sue had been there. 'And it may fit, Tom. Franklin told me that the Arabs need about two thousand new falcons every autumn. It's a multi-million-pound business. And when you think of the number which probably die in transit – it's horrible. Some smugglers even stitch the birds' eyelids in transit.'

'And you think Thieron may have passed on the bird to this Mahkted?'

'It would be a way of cutting his losses.'

'What time is the plane due to leave?'

Caines glanced at his watch. 'About forty-five minutes from now.'

Tom stared at him. 'We might be able to get there in time.'

'Yes,' said Caines. 'Let's give it a damn good try, shall we?'

Caines's car was parked outside. He drove as fast as safety allowed to the airport, but time was against them. As they drove down the approach road, they saw a light aircraft lift from the runway, heading south. Caines checked his watch: it was Mahkted's flight.

He pulled the car over.

'Well,' said Tom, 'that's a pity.'

'And we'll never know, will we?'

'While we're here we might as well check their flight plans for the last couple of years. See if it's a regular thing.'

'Good idea,' said Caines. 'I hadn't thought of that.'

The two men got out of the car and walked towards the airport buildings. Nearby, a man sitting in a white Mercedes was watching them through binoculars.

'Well, well,' Charles Thieron said to the woman sitting beside him. 'It is fortunate that we came to see Sammy off. Our Customs friends are becoming inquisitive again, and he only just got away in time.' Thieron gave a small sigh. 'This Mr Caines is proving to be a nuisance, and your inside knowledge of Customs might be very useful to us.'

'And if it is,' said the woman, 'you will reward me suitably?'

Thieron turned to her. 'Of course. You know I will do almost anything for you, my dear Annie.'

Annie Soldstrom smiled, and she leaned forward to receive Thieron's kiss.

# *Chapter Fifteen*

'Aly's late,' Nigel remarked to Bruce a few days later.

'Very late,' he agreed. It was approaching ten A.M.

'Perhaps Thomas is acting up,' Nigel suggested.

Bruce tapped his biro against his chin, looking thoughtful.

'How does she seem to you?' Nigel asked.

'Fragile. She's been holding herself together these past few days, but it's not easy for her. And little wonder.'

A yachtsman entered the Long Room, and Nigel attended to him. Afterwards he returned to the telephone directory he had been perusing. Tom Gibbons had asked him to find some bedsitter addresses, and Nigel was only too eager to oblige. It was he, after all, who had been the unwitting pawn in the break-up of Tom and Sue's marriage; it was the least he could do.

The internal telephone rang, and Nigel picked it up.

'Nigel,' said Harry Caines, 'could you ask Alyson to come to my office, please.'

'Uh,' said Nigel, 'she's not here at the moment, sir.'

'Where is she?'

'I think she's just stepped outside.'

'Well, when she comes back, tell her I'd like to see her.'

Nigel put the receiver down, aware that Bruce was staring at him disapprovingly.

'She's bound to turn up soon,' Nigel said defensively.

'It was a fib, Nigel. You should have told Caines that she hasn't arrived yet.'

'And drop Aly right in it?'

'You know Caines. He's not going to like it if he finds out you've been covering up for her.'

'She'll be here soon,' Nigel insisted, though less confidently than before.

Bruce rose from his desk. 'We don't know that, Nigel.'

'Where are you going?'

'To tell Caines that Aly hasn't come in yet.'

He went out. Nigel was mortified, but Bruce was his superior and there was nothing he could do. He stared anxiously at the doorway, expecting Bruce to return with a furious Caines who would tear a strip off him.

But Bruce returned alone. Nigel glowered at him and muttered, 'Judas.'

Bruce was unruffled. 'Your loyalty's misplaced, Nigel. You're not helping Aly.'

'She's going through a rough period. You needn't have shopped her.'

'It's precisely because she's going through a rough period that it's important we keep an eye on her. Caines agreed with me.'

'That must have pleased you no end.'

'I wasn't trying to curry favour, or get you into trouble. I was thinking of Aly. We have to make sure that she's all right. It's just not like her to be late, and perhaps something's wrong.'

This had not really occurred to Nigel.

'Shall I give her a ring?' he asked.

'Caines has already tried telephoning her cottage. There was no answer.'

'So what do we do?'

'*We* get on with our work. Caines is driving out to the cottage right now.'

It was a bright, clear morning, but Calvin wasn't in a sunny mood. He sat on the towpath beside the river near his cottage, staring at Annie's yacht, which was moored nearby. Annie herself wasn't around. She had left a message at the cottage the previous evening to say that she was visiting a woman friend in Southampton. He had expected her to arrive back sometime late in the night, but she hadn't appeared and he felt hopelessly abandoned.

Damn it, Cal, he told himself, if she's left her yacht here, she must be coming back. He had never felt such a longing for a woman before, never felt so anxious and uncertain of himself.

Lying back on the grassy bank, he pulled his cap down over his eyes and tried to relax and enjoy the sunshine. He was due on duty at the Custom House in an hour's time, but he was hoping that Annie would appear before he left.

A gentle breeze rustled the tall grass, and everything around him was tranquil. But Calvin himself simply could not relax, and finally he rose and made his way back to the cottage.

His Renault 5 was parked outside. He was about to climb into it when a yellow Volvo turned down the approach. It was the car Annie had hired for herself, and his spirits soared. But at the same time he felt angry with her.

She pulled up alongside him and got out of the car.

'Calvin,' she said, smiling her perfect white smile. 'It is a beautiful morning, *ja*?'

'All right for some,' he said grumpily. 'Where have you been?'

'Been? In Southampton with my friend Greta, of course. I do not see her for many years, and so we have much to talk about. We also drink the wines she makes now she is living here in England – elderberry wine, I think it is, and some made from turnips. Foof! Soon we are both giddy and laughing, then sleepy. So I spend the night on her sofa.'

To Calvin, she looked radiant, but he resisted the urge to hug her.

'You might have phoned.'

'I am sorry. Greta and I – we have much news to catch up on. Then it is so late and we are so drunk that we sleep. But in the morning I think of my Calvin and I know I must make it up to you. So I bring you this –'

She reached into the pocket of her windcheater and produced a small package wrapped in tissue paper.

Calvin took it from her and peeled back the paper. Then he took the lid off the box. Inside was a Rolex Oyster wristwatch.

'I buy it in a jewellers in Southampton before I leave this morning,' she told him. 'And later I will treat you to lunch, *ja*?'

Calvin began to grin with joy and delight.

'Come here,' he said, pulling her to him and planting a huge kiss on her lips.

As Caines approached Alyson's cottage, he saw Thomas tied to a fence in the paddock. The horse looked somehow abandoned.

He drove quickly up to the front of the house and got out of the car. The cottage door was open.

'Alyson?' Caines called, going inside.

The living room was empty. He went into the bedroom, but she was not there, either. The bed had not been made.

He went back outside. The cottage was surrounded by pastureland, but there was no sign of Alyson in the fields. He called her name again, but still there was no reply.

Beyond the paddock was a small oak copse. Alyson had mentioned that she sometimes watered Thomas at the stream which ran through its centre. He walked towards it.

Caines heard the sounds of sobbing moments after entering the copse. Alyson was sitting in the dappled sunlight on a moss-covered log beside the stream. She was staring bleakly into the water, tears trickling down her cheeks.

Caines sat down beside her and put an arm around her shoulder. Her response to this was to burst into full blooded tears. He held on to her, saying nothing, waiting for the flood of sorrow to run its course.

Finally she subsided into silence. Head turned away from

him, she whispered, 'I'm sorry.'

'Don't be. It had to come sooner or later.'

She took a handkerchief from the pocket of her jacket and wiped the tears from her cheeks. She wore her Customs uniform, her hair neatly tied up under her hat.

'I was ready to come in,' she said, 'then suddenly I couldn't move. Suddenly it all come pouring out of me.' She turned to look at him, despair on her face. 'What am I going to do, Harry? I feel as if my life has come to an end.'

'It hasn't,' he said gently. 'Believe me, it hasn't. But it's natural to feel that way. You can only keep grief buried for so long, then it comes bubbling up.'

'I've lost it all – my enthusiasm, my drive, my ambition. I can't go through with Wembley – I can't face it.'

'Yes you can. With help.'

She shook her head vehemently. 'I've only got a few days. It's too much. I can't see the point in anything any more.'

Caines was silent for a moment. Then he said, 'I felt the same way too, after I lost my family. To start with, you try to deny all your feelings, you try to keep going. Then it catches up with you.'

She nodded. 'It's like a dam bursting.'

'It's also like a bruise coming out. It begins the process of healing, even though you may not think so at the time. You have to feel terrible for a while before you can start to feel better.'

Alyson stared down again at the water trickling by in the stream, sunlight flashing on it.

'At the moment,' she said, 'I feel as if I'm never going to get my life together again.'

'You will,' he insisted. 'But it's at times like these that you have to rely on the help of friends. I made the mistake of trying to shoulder it all myself. That's why it took me so long to get over what had happened. I sometimes think I never quite managed it completely.'

She peered at him; he had never talked of his family before.

'You still think of them a lot?' she asked.

'There isn't an hour that goes by when I don't. I even dream about them occasionally.'

'Bad dreams?'

He shook his head. 'It's only bad when I wake and realize that they're not really there. But you have to give yourself something else to live for. And the Foxhunter could help you. You can't spoil my plans now.'

Again she looked at him. 'Spoil your plans? What do you mean?'

'You want someone to help you with Thomas, don't you? Mucking out, and all that stuff. Well, I'm offering my services.'

'Are you serious?'

'Of course I am. I've already arranged my leave-days so that I can be with you at Wembley, and I'll help out in my spare time before then. I may not know anything about horses, but that just means you're going to have to train me, doesn't it? So you'd better start getting yourself organized.'

Alyson could hardly believe what she was hearing. She knew Caines was being serious, and she also knew he was deliberately bullying her out of her grief and self-pity. And it was working. She suddenly felt that with his help she might be able to see it through.

'Well?' said Caines. 'Is it a deal?'

She hesitated, then said, 'It's a deal.'

'Good. I won't expect you in today. Use your time to give Thomas a bit of practice, yes? I'll expect to see him spick and span when I come back this evening. Then you can start showing me the ropes.'

Tom Gibbons was at his desk when Calvin entered, whistling.

'You're cheerful,' he remarked dourly.

'It's the weather,' Calvin replied. But it was, in fact, Annie. Her reappearance, and the Rolex she had bought him, had restored all his confidence and good-humour.

'Cal,' said Tom, 'I want to ask you something.'

'Ask away.'

'When you went to Thieron's place to impound the Gyr-falcon, was there anyone else at the house with him?'

Calvin was caught off balance. 'Why do you ask?'

'I had a feeling you and Caines were keeping something from me. So I phoned Franklin in Bristol half an hour ago and asked him about what had happened. He let slip that there had been a woman there who was the wife of a Customs officer.'

Calvin did not know what to say.

'It was Sue, wasn't it?'

Calvin could see that Tom was trying to remain calm and reasonable. He remained silent.

'Was it?' Tom demanded.

'Yes.'

'Then why didn't anyone tell me?'

'It was for your own sake, Tom. We thought it might cloud the issue.'

'For my own sake! I think you should allow me to be the judge of that. She's my wife, Cal!'

Calvin shrugged. 'You're not living together any more.'

'Thanks for reminding me!'

'No – I mean that as far as Sue's probably concerned, she's a free agent –'

'Has she been hanging around Thieron for long?'

'I don't know.'

'But she was with him at the house when you and Caines turned up?'

'She was around, yes.'

'And you didn't tell me. So much for friendship.'

'It's because we're friends that I didn't, Tom. We're closing on Thieron and we might be able to get him without involving Sue. But if you go charging in there, you might ruin everything.'

Tom was only half-listening. He had already risen and was taking his coat off the back of the chair.

'I'm happy to leave Thieron to you,' he said. 'It's Sue I want to see. If she's messing around with Thieron, it may give me the lever I need to make sure that she can't stop me from seeing the children.'

This had not occurred to Calvin. He tried to put himself in Tom's position, and he realized he would probably react in the same way.

'So what are you going to do?' he asked.

'I'm going to go to my father-in-law and demand to see her. Then I'll tell her what I know. Make her see reason about the kids. My whole life's in pieces, Cal. You've got to help me salvage what I can.'

Calvin knew this was very risky, but he could not have denied Tom for a moment. 'What do you want me to do?'

'Lend me your car.'

Calvin paused for a moment before delving into his jacket pocket and tossing the keys on to Tom's desk. Tom picked them up and went out without a further word.

He drove out of Wrelling to the Langley house, telling himself that he had to keep calm, keep his emotions under control. But inside he was seething. As he turned down the driveway, he saw Sue emerging from the house, and all his anger came bubbling to the surface.

She had opened the door of her Sierra, but she paused as Tom drew up alongside her. Her father was standing on the doorstep, watching both of them.

'Well, well,' she said as Tom got out of Calvin's Renault. 'Look what the cat's dragged in. Calvin lend you his car?'

'I want a word with you,' Tom said. 'I know about you and Thieron.'

'Know? What do you know?'

'You were at his house with him when Caines and the others took the falcon.'

She shrugged. 'So what if I was?'

'You're having an affair with him, aren't you?'

'That's none of your damn business!'

'Oh yes it is. It's very much my business. You think you're going to keep the children away from me, but the divorce courts will take a great interest in the fact that you've been sleeping with a criminal.'

Sue simply stared at him, contempt in her face. 'God, you're so pathetic. There's one thing I will say about Charles – he's twice the man you are.'

Before Tom could say anything further she got into the car, slamming the door behind her. The key was in the ignition, and she turned it and revved the engine before reversing the car so swiftly that Tom had to jump out of the way.

He watched her drive off at speed, feeling that somehow he had lost the initiative once more, failed to press home his advantage. Jack Langley was regarding him from the doorway of the house.

'You never learn, do you, Tom? You won't get your way with Sue by trying to bully her.'

'I was just stating the facts,' Tom said.

'Maybe you were, but it makes no difference. Sue's like her mother – flattery's the only way to get round them. Flattery and cosseting. You have to give them what they want. Then they'll behave.'

Tom made to get back in Calvin's car.

'Listen,' Jack said, 'there's only one way of making sure you don't lose the kids. You and Sue have to get back together.'

'I'm not interested. And she wouldn't be if I was.'

'I think she would if she knew you could support her in the manner to which she's accustomed.'

'Meaning?'

'Take the job I've offered. It's the last time I'll ask. Take it, and you'll have Sue beating a path to your door again in no time at all. What do you say?'

'Stuff it,' said Tom.

'I'm covering for Tom,' Calvin told Bruce and Nigel. 'He should be back in an hour, but in the meantime, if Caines should ask where he is – well, fudge it, all right?'

Nigel glanced pointedly at Bruce, who said, 'Sorry, Cal, but if you're asking me to lie, I can't.'

'Lie? Who said anything about lying? Tom's got personal problems and he's gone off to try to sort them out. I just want you to cover for him, that's all.'

'Sorry, Cal,' Bruce said again. 'But I think it's wrong. Caines should be kept informed of what's going on.'

Calvin's temper flared. 'You'll do as you're told, Bruce. Perhaps you've forgotten that I'm the HEO around here. You'll cover for Tom as I've asked.'

'That won't be necessary,' said the voice of Harry Caines.

Calvin spun around, and Caines walked into the Long Room.

'We won't be needing any subterfuge, gentlemen, since I've gathered from the gist of your conversation what's going on. Calvin, my office immediately.'

Caines departed as quickly as he had come, leaving Calvin wondering just how much he had overheard. He glared at Bruce, then went down the corridor to Caines's office, steeling himself for a roasting.

But Caines did not look angry. 'Take a seat,' he told Calvin.

'I'm sorry, sir,' Calvin managed to mutter.

'Under other circumstances I'd take a dimmer view of your behaviour. But Tom *is* in trouble, and I sympathize with your attempt to help him – misguided though it is.'

'He knows about his wife being at Thieron's, sir. He asked me straight out, and I couldn't lie to him. He's gone to see her.'

'I gathered something like that must have happened.'

'He's promised to lay off Thieron, but it might muddy our pitch anyway. I think his main concern is with losing his children.'

'That's understandable, but it makes our work more difficult.' Caines looked contemplative, then sighed. 'Tom's in an impossible position. And the longer it goes on, the more his wife is likely to compromise him.'

'That's very true.'

'So what would you advise?'

'Advise? What exactly do you mean, sir?'

'We have to consider Tom's future. It's obvious he can't continue as he's been doing. I think it would be best for him if he was transferred to another District. What's your opinion? You've known him longer than the rest of us.'

Calvin considered, then said, 'It would probably be for the best, sir. As much as I'd hate to see him go.'

'Good. I'll speak to the Assistant Collector and arrange an interview for Tom. And I think it's time I had a word with his wife as well.'

The crack of a gunshot sent rooks scattering from a row of larches which flanked the driveway. Sue Gibbons jumped at the sound as she climbed out of her car.

The shot had come from the direction of the grounds behind Charles Thieron's mansion. Sue followed the curving pathway around the side of the house to the large pond which lay beyond. Thieron was standing near the water's edge, lining up his next shot. Ducks swam in line on the water, seemingly unaware of their peril.

'Charles!' she called, hurrying towards him.

Thieron smiled on seeing her. He lowered his shotgun and kissed her on the cheek, saying, 'Sue, my darling. What brings you here so unexpectedly?'

Sue had intended to go shopping for a new dress when

Tom had turned up outside her father's house. Instead she had driven straight to Thieron's.

She gave him the gist of her conversation with Tom. Thieron listened with a faint smile on his lips. When she was finished, he merely shrugged.

'It is nothing,' he told her. 'He is simply a wounded man, striking out in his pain.'

'But he called you a criminal, Charles.'

'That is what many men call those few who are not timid and who take their opportunities boldly. I have been called such things before. It is of no consequence.'

'But he's threatened to use my friendship with you to make sure that he gets the children. If there's a divorce, he'll try to involve you as the third party.'

Thieron shook his head. 'You must not worry – it will not come to that. I have met men like your husband before. They are full of sound and fury, signifying nothing. He cannot harm us.'

'Are you sure, Charles? Don't forget he's a Customs officer.'

Thieron put an arm around her shoulder. 'Trust me, my dear Sue. Nothing will come of it. You are safe here now, with me, are you not? It is a glorious day, so let us enjoy it.'

There was something about his presence which always reassured her. He radiated security, strength and power, and his arm around her was like a shield which would protect her from everything.

Then he stepped back and raised his shotgun once more. The ducks floated on the pond, unsuspecting. She braced herself for the sound of the shot.

'Mr Caines,' said Jack Langley. 'This is an unexpected pleasure.'

The servant who had answered the door had led Caines through the house to the verandah where Jack was sitting, a brandy in his hand.

Caines said, 'I'm afraid it's business, not pleasure, Mr Langley. I wanted to have a word with your daughter.'

'She's out. Left an hour ago.'

'Do you happen to know where she's gone?'

Jack lit a cigar. 'Not a clue. Or when she'll be back. If you'd telephoned, I might have been able to save you the journey.'

Caines shrugged. 'It's a nice day for driving. Perhaps you can help me instead.'

Jack peered up at him without speaking. Then he turned to the servant, who was still hovering beside Caines.

'Fetch Mr Caines a drink,' he said. 'What would you like?'

'I'll have a Perrier water, please,' said Caines.

He sat down at the table with Jack, who was contemplating his cigar. Curlicues of blue smoke wreathed his head.

Neither man said anything until the servant had returned with Caines's Perrier water and departed again.

'You teetotal?' Jack asked.

'I'm partial to scotch on special occasions,' Caines told him. 'But not when I'm working.'

'I remember my father telling me never to trust a man who didn't drink. Mind you, he was a boozer *and* a rogue.'

Caines sensed that Langley was offering an olive branch of some sort to him. He said, 'Do you know about your daughter's association with Charles Thieron?'

Langley nodded slowly through a haze of smoke. 'I know about it, yes.'

'And do you approve?'

'Depends what you're asking me to approve of, doesn't it?'

'Does she realize the risks she's running?'

'Risks?'

'Let's be frank, Mr Langley – Charles Thieron is a dangerous man to be involved with.'

'What do you mean – dangerous?'

Caines took a mouthful of mineral water. 'Did you hear about the white falcon we confiscated from him?'

'Sue mentioned something about it.'

'It was later stolen. Two men broke into a wildlife sanctuary where the falcon was being held. They coshed a man of sixty-eight to get the bird. He's in hospital with concussion. It could have been far worse.'

Caines allowed the implications to sink in. Langley said, 'Are you telling me it was Thieron's doing?'

'We have no concrete proof that it was. But what would you assume? I'm sure you know that Mr Thieron likes to get his own way in his business dealings. I just wanted you to be aware of the lengths to which he may be capable of going.'

Langley puffed hard on his cigar, staring out over the lawn.

'So what are you trying to say?' he asked.

'I think you should put pressure to bear on your daughter to stay away from him. He's flirting dangerously with the laws of this country, and if he oversteps himself he'll be in deep trouble. And if that happens, he could drag others down with him. Your daughter, for example.'

Langley was silent for a moment. Then he said. 'Is Sue's welfare your only concern?'

'No,' Caines admitted, 'I'm thinking of Tom as well. He's being gravely compromised by your daughter's behaviour. But she's at risk, too. She should be made aware that she's playing a very serious game with Charles Thieron.'

The restaurant was a small, intimate place overlooking the harbour. Calvin and Annie shared a bottle of hock with their lunch, and Annie kept Calvin entertained with a variety of fictitious anecdotes about her visit to Greta's in Southampton. Greta did not in fact exist, and she had spent the night with Charles Thieron, planning the pick-up of the cannabis shipment which would be arriving in a matter of days.

Calvin's gullibility amused her. She knew he had a reputation as a lady-killer who had often cajoled women with expensive presents. He couldn't see that she had turned the tables on him, placating him with the Rolex Oyster. The watch had cost her nothing: it had been given her by Charles and was actually part of a shipment which had been smuggled into the country several weeks before. The irony pleased her. Calvin was like a puppy dog, and she simply had to keep tossing him the occasional bone in order to keep him happy. He had no inkling that she was one of Charles's most trusted couriers, and had been for many years.

Jack Langley sat on the verandah for most of the afternoon, thinking. A servant brought his lunch on a tray to the table, but he ate little of it. Caines's visit had given him pause for thought. He had no particular liking for Customs officials, but the Surveyor struck him as a man whose integrity he could respect.

Sue arrived back at four-thirty, and she sought him out on the verandah.

'Where've you been?' he asked.

She immediately bristled. 'Why?'

'Someone was here to see you.'

'Oh? Who?'

'Harry Caines from Customs.'

She sat down at the table, affecting to be unconcerned. A servant brought her a long tumbler of orange juice packed with ice. Jack waited, knowing his daughter.

'Where are the kids?' she asked.

'Connie's taken them to the beach. You should spend more time with them, Sue.'

She raised the glass to her lips and drank at length, not looking at him.

'What did Caines want?' she asked finally.

'He came here to warn you off Charles Thieron. For your

own sake. He says Thieron's a dangerous man.'

Again she bristled. 'And did you tell him to mind his own business?'

'As a matter of fact, I didn't. I happen to think that he's right.'

She jumped up angrily. 'Why is it that everyone else seems to know what's best for me? Why can't they leave me alone to live my life as I damn well see fit!'

'Sue –' Jack began, but his daughter had already stormed off.

Jack sighed, and watched a blackbird struggling to remove a worm from the lawn. Then he rose from the table and went inside to the drawing room. Closing the door behind him, he picked up the telephone and punched out Charles Thieron's number.

A servant at the other end answered, and Jack asked to speak to Thieron personally. At length he heard the Frenchman say, 'Jack, how are you?'

'I'm fine, Charles,' Jack replied, his tone serious. 'But I'm afraid I've got some bad news.'

'Oh?'

'The arrangement we discussed about you taking over some of my business interests. . .'

'Yes?'

'Well, I've decided against it. The deal's off.'

# *Chapter Sixteen*

'Ah,' said Charles Christie, 'come inside, Tom. Have a seat.'

Tom Gibbons closed the door behind him and sat down on the chair in front of the Assistant Collector's desk.

'Would you like some tea?' Christie asked.

'No thanks.'

'Coffee?'

'I'm fine, sir.'

Christie nodded and did not bother ordering any for himself. Caines had only informed Tom the previous morning that he had arranged an interview for him with the AC, and he had not been forthcoming on its purpose. Secretly Tom had begun to hope that he was going to be offered promotion, and during the train ride to Southampton he had tried to imagine how this might change his life. The rise in salary would mean that at least he could afford to rent a better place than the rather miserable bedsitter which Nigel had found for him yesterday.

Christie shuffled a few papers on his desk, then said, 'How have things been going with you lately, Tom? I was sorry to hear about the problems you've had at home, and I thought it might be useful if we had this chat.'

Tom was immediately put on the defensive. 'I'm managing, sir.'

'I gather Harry Caines has taken you under his wing temporarily, so to speak. A spare bedroom, yes?'

'I've found a place of my own now, sir. I'll be moving in immediately.'

'Good,' Christie said, somewhat remotely. 'So how have you been coping? Getting along all right with Harry

Caines?'

'We've had our ups and downs, sir, as I'm sure you're aware. But things are fine now.'

'Really? I'm glad to hear that.'

But Christie sounded sceptical, and Tom felt deeply uneasy. The Assistant Collector stroked the sparse hair on his head. He looked slightly discomfited, as if he was trying to think of a tactful way to broach a delicate subject.

'It seems to me,' he said at last, 'that you're in a rather difficult position in Wrelling now, Tom. I gather that your wife has formed a friendship with a Frenchman who's had a few run-ins with our officers –'

'I don't see what that has to do with me.'

'It has everything to do with you, Tom. It's compromising you.'

'I can't be held responsible for my wife's behaviour now that we're no longer together.'

'Agreed. But nevertheless its consequences still affect you directly.'

'So what are you proposing I do about it?'

'I think it would be in your best interests if we considered transferring you to another District.'

Tom was not prepared for this. He stared at Christie, thinking furiously.

'Was this Harry Caines's idea?' he asked.

'He thinks it would be best for you. And I agree.'

'I see. And this transfer – are we talking about a promotion, sir?'

'Under the present circumstances I don't think that would really be appropriate. But when the dust has settled –'

Tom surged to his feet, feeling wounded and betrayed. All the resentment which he had felt for Harry Caines had returned. He was being punished for Sue's behaviour, being made a scapegoat.

'I'll tell you what I think of the transfer idea,' he said to

Christie, 'I think it stinks. And you stink too – the whole lot of you. To hell with the bloody job!'

He stormed out.

Calvin walked along the towpath towards Annie's yacht. She was on board, and had risen early that morning to get the boat shipshape for a trip along the coast to Dartmouth.

Calvin crept on board stealthily. Annie was crouching with her back to him, oiling a line of galvanized wire. He tiptoed up to her, then flung his arms around her waist, saying, 'Boo!'

Annie jumped and spun around.

'Calvin!' she said, her blue eyes sparkling. 'You nearly give me the heart attack.'

'Morning, my beauty. You're up bright and early.'

'I am checking the yacht for tomorrow.'

Calvin stared around the boat. Annie had certainly been thorough in her preparations – she was even airing the storm sails.

'Expecting bad weather?' he asked her

'The forecast is good, but it is better to be prepared, no? At sea you must take no chances.'

Annie had told him that she ran an antiques business in Stockholm, and she was making the trip to Dartmouth to look for china and glassware. Calvin had a rest-day tomorrow, and he would have loved to accompany her. But she had hinted that she preferred to go alone.

'What time will you be leaving?' he asked.

'With the early tide.'

'Are you sure you don't want company?'

'It is better I go alone. I like to spend many hours searching for objects of interest in the shops. You would be bored.'

'With you, never.'

'You would distract me.'

'You bet I would!'

'And then I make the bad purchases. No, I must go alone.'

'But you'll be back the same day?'

'Yes, but it will be late. Do not wait up for me. I will creep into your bed when you do not expect it.'

Calvin grinned. 'How about creeping down below with me right now? I've still got half an hour before I go in.'

'Calvin!' Annie said, as though shocked by the suggestion. But her eyes were filled with mischief.

Seated at his desk, Harry Caines inspected a broken fingernail and reflected that Alyson was a stern taskmaster. Tomorrow she would be riding in the Foxhunter, and for the past few evening Caines had been going to her cottage to help her with Thomas. He and Thomas had struck up an immediate rapport, which was just as well, for there was a lot to be learned. Grooming alone involved using a variety of different brushes, then there were sponges for cleaning the eyes, nose and dock, combs for untangling the mane and tail, a rubber for giving the coat a final polish, and so on. He had spent much of his time up to his knees in mud and straw, trying to avoid playful kicks from Thomas as he picked stones and caked manure from his feet. It was hard and exhausting work, and Alyson had been quite sharp with him whenever he was less than totally diligent. Caines didn't mind this in the slightest, for it was an indication that she was beginning to come to terms with the loss of Chris Lucas.

The telephone rang, and Caines picked it up.

'Caines,' he said.

'Harry, this is Charles Christie. Bad news. I talked to Tom Gibbons, and he's just charged out of here. Wouldn't accept the idea of a transfer for a moment. He told me to go to hell.'

Caines sighed, closing his eyes.

'You're going to need another HEO, Harry.'

'Did he resign?'

'His parting words were "To hell with the bloody job!" I think that's pretty unambiguous, don't you?'

Caines shook his head in dismay. 'He's a fool to himself.'

'He let his temper get the better of him, Harry. Well, there's nothing we can do. I suggest you get one of your people as acting HEO. Any suggestions?'

Caines did not have to consider long.

'Bruce Tomlin, sir,' he said.

'Good idea,' Christie said immediately. 'He's intelligent and reliable. Give me a call when it's confirmed.'

Christie rang off. Caines sat there for a while, thinking about Tom and wondering what, if anything, he could do to help. He had feared that Tom might take umbrage to the suggestion of a transfer, but he had not anticipated that his reaction would be so violent.

Rising from his desk, he went down the corridor to the Long Room. Nigel, Alyson and Bruce were all on duty.

'If Tom comes in,' Caines said to them, 'ask him to come and see me. In the meantime I'd like to have a word with you, Bruce.'

There was something in Caines's tone which made Alyson and Nigel suspect that all was not well. And when Bruce returned from Caines's office twenty minutes later, he looked shocked.

'What's happened?' Alyson asked him.

'Tom's resigned. Or at least it appears he has. He walked out of an interview with the Assistant Collector.'

Alyson and Nigel looked at one another, then at Bruce.

'That's all Caines told me,' Bruce said. 'Tom hasn't appeared?'

They both shook their heads.

'There's more. I'm going to be standing in for Tom.'

It took a moment for this to sink in.

'You've been promoted?' Alyson said.

'I suppose so. It's temporary at the moment. Secondment.'

'You don't sound very happy about it,' Nigel remarked.

Bruce shrugged. 'You know me. I've been quite content just drifting along. In a way I'm pleased, but in a way I'm not. Particularly since it seems to be at Tom's expense.'

'Don't be daft,' said Alyson. 'You had it coming anyway, Bruce. It's a shame about Tom, but that wasn't your fault.'

'I suppose not. Caines did say that he'd recommended me on merit.'

'There you are then. Good for you.'

Nigel saluted him. 'Does that mean we'll have to call you "sir" from now on?'

'That's right,' Bruce said dolefully, 'rub it in.'

'What do you think Tom's going to do?' Alyson asked.

'I hope he comes to his senses,' Bruce replied. 'It's such a waste to throw away his whole career.'

Calvin entered, having just arrived. They told him what had happened.

Calvin was stunned by the news, and it took him a moment to recover.

'I'm pleased for you, Bruce,' he said. 'But I'm damned sorry for Tom. Anyone know where he is?'

Nigel said, 'He may be at that new bedsitter I found him.'

'Have you got a telephone number?' Calvin asked.

'There's no phone. He wanted a place without one.'

'That sounds bad,' Bruce remarked. 'As if he wants to shut himself off from the world. Caines has tried to ring him at his own flat, but there's no reply.'

'Do you think,' Nigel began, 'do you think it was my fault? You know, that misunderstanding with Sue. I can't help feeling guilty.'

'Don't overestimate your importance,' Calvin told him. 'Sue was restless long before she snared you in her web. And now she's hanging around Thieron. The break-up would have come sooner or later. Give me the address of Tom's new place, will you? I think I'll pay him a visit this evening.'

Nigel found the address, and Calvin made a note of it. The mood in the Long Room was now solemn, subdued. In an effort to lighten it, Alyson reached into her shoulderbag and produced three tickets which she offered to the others.

'What are these?' Nigel asked.

'Tickets for Wembley tomorrow,' she told him. 'They'll get you into the competitors' enclosure. I hope you're all coming.'

Both Nigel and Bruce were enthusiastic, whereas Calvin stared at his ticket dubiously.

'What's the matter, Cal?' Alyson asked him. 'Can't you make it?'

Calvin was not on duty, but he was still hoping to persuade Annie to let him accompany her on the trip to Dartmouth.

'I'm not sure I can,' he said vaguely. 'Something has come up.'

He could see the disappointment on Alyson's face and he immediately relented.

'No,' he said, 'it's not important. I'll be there.'

She had been shopping and had bought herself several new outfits; but still she felt restless and dissatisfied. Sue Gibbons turned her Sierra down the approach road to Charles Thieron's mansion, having decided at the last moment to call in on him.

The front door of the mansion was slightly ajar, so she walked inside without ringing the bell. There was no one about. She went into the drawing room, expecting to find Charles there. But it was empty.

She enjoyed the feeling of having entered the house without anyone knowing. Charles's Mercedes was parked outside, so he had to be at home. She would simply wait until he walked in.

The grandfather clock beside the window ticked loudly,

steadily. Five minutes passed. She went over to the drinks cabinet and poured herself a glass of white wine which she diluted with soda. At this point a blonde woman in her thirties walked into the room.

Both women were equally surprised to see one another. Sue immediately resented the other woman's appearance, and she was determined to impose her authority over her.

'I'm Sue Gibbons,' she said. 'You are?'

'Annie. Annie Soldstrom.'

'Well, Annie, is Charles here?'

'He is here, yes. You wish to see him?'

'I would hardly be here if I didn't, would I?'

Sue thought she detected a flicker of irritation in the woman's face. Then Charles himself walked in.

'Sue,' he said, his face breaking into a smile. 'What an unexpected pleasure.' He glanced at Annie, then said, 'Have you two ladies been getting to know one another?'

'We've only just met,' Sue said, a hint of suspicion in her voice.

'Ah,' said Thieron. Then he turned to Annie. 'My dear, I think perhaps our client will be arriving soon. Perhaps you would like to go and prepare yourself.'

He spoke as though addressing a rather dimwitted child. The woman glanced at Sue, then said, 'Yes, Charles. I will go now.'

She left the room without closing the door behind her.

'Who's she?' Sue asked, still suspicious.

Thieron shrugged. 'Just another of the girls. A business acquaintance from Germany requires company for a trip to South Africa. He selected her.'

She frowned at him. 'Sometimes, Charles, I think you treat women like cattle.'

He shook his head calmly. 'I am simply the middle-man, Sue. The girls offer their services quite freely, and I arrange good terms for them. They all have expensive habits, and they are well paid for the duties they perform. But you should not fret on that score. You are in a different class altogether.'

He took her hand, smiled at her.

'So she's just that? Another of your girls?'

'I assure you.'

He drew her to him and kissed her forehead.

'She's nothing,' he whispered. 'And soon she will be gone.'

Reassurance flooded through her. At first she had had a suspicion that the woman was close to him, but he had dispelled her anxiety.

'Charles,' she said, 'I need a holiday.'

He nodded. 'This is perhaps a good time for it. You will join your mother in Marbella?'

'No. I want to go away with you. Can't we just take the cruiser somewhere? Or fly to the Caribbean? I'm bored, and I need a break.'

Thieron spread his arms in a gesture to indicate that he regretted being unable to oblige.

'Alas,' he said, 'I have important business to conduct here.'

'What's so important that it can't wait for a few days? A fortnight, that's all I'm asking for, Charles – or even a week. Let's go away for just a week.'

He shook his head. 'I wish it was possible. But it is not.'

Now Sue's frustration began to turn to anger. 'I'm beginning to think that you don't want to be with me, Charles.'

'It is not that.'

'Then prove it. Let's go away today.'

Suddenly Annie Soldstrom walked in, holding a cordless telephone. She had been listening outside the door ever since Thieron had given her the hint that she was to behave just like one of his high-class tarts. He had warned her previously that Sue Gibbons had a habit of dropping in unexpectedly on him, and they had rehearsed the procedure before, just in case. There was no client from Germany, of course, and she had been intimate with Charles for many years. And now she was going to rescue him from this pestering woman.

'Charles,' she said, 'it is a telephone call from a man in Boggy Regis, I think it is, who says you must go there this afternoon to see a shipment he has for you. He says the hold is full of firelighters, not cigars.'

Thieron took the phone from her. The line was dead, but he made a good show of pretending to be angry with the 'man' at its other end while Sue watched him, perplexed. Finally he slammed down the phone.

'I am sorry, Sue,' he said, 'but I must leave immediately. I am a victim of an act of incompetence, and it is necessary for me to make a personal demonstration of my disapproval.' To Annie he said, 'I will be gone for the rest of the day. You know what to do when our client arrives?'

She nodded.

Sue rose. 'When will you be back, Charles?'

'Tomorrow, I promise. Then we will go away together. Antigua, perhaps? I have a small villa there.'

'Sounds wonderful!'

He kissed her on the cheek. Mollified, she departed. As soon as Annie heard the door closing, she burst into laughter.

Thieron put a hand over her mouth to stifle the sounds, but he was also amused.

'Boggy Regis,' he said. 'That was ludicrous, Annie.'

'But it worked,' she said.

'Yes,' he agreed, watching from the window as Sue got into her car and drove away. 'She is a foolish young thing. It is no better than she deserved.'

'And tomorrow, Charles? Will you take her to Antigua?'

'Tomorrow we have bigger fish to fry, my dear Annie, do we not? I will avoid her.'

She gave him a teasing look. 'And now?'

'Now,' he said, 'it is time for a little pleasure before

business.'

They kissed.

'I'll be at the cottage in an hour,' Caines told Alyson as they left the Custom House together at six o'clock. 'I'm going home first to see if Tom's there.'

Alyson nodded gravely. 'I hope he's all right.'

'It's probably his dignity that's been most hurt. I just hope that he'll listen to reason.'

'What are you going to say to him?'

'All I can do is remind him of the options he has. In the end, it's his life and he has to make his own decisions about it.'

They walked outside to Alyson's car.

'By the way,' Caines remarked casually, 'there's something waiting for you at home. A present, for tomorrow.'

'What is it?'

'You'll find out when you get there.'

'Don't I even get a hint?'

'It's big and inanimate.'

Her curiosity was aroused, and she pressed him. But he wouldn't give her any hints. Finally she got into her car and drove off. Caines walked the short distance to his flat.

As he was unlocking the door, some intuition was telling him that Tom had already moved out. And so it proved. The door to the bedroom he had been using was open and the room was empty inside, the bed neatly made. Tom had brought few belongings with him to the flat, and these were all gone.

Caines went out again. His car was parked outside. He got into it and drove away, heading for the address of Tom's new bedsitter which he had obtained from Nigel.

A few minutes later he pulled up outside a dilapidated Victorian mansion which had been converted into flats. An untrimmed privet hedge spilled over a squat brick wall, and the flagstone path leading up to the front door was cracked and uneven. As Caines climbed out of his car, he saw Calvin standing in the doorway, vainly pressing one of the doorbells on the jamb.

'There's no answer,' he said to Caines. 'I've been ringing for the past five minutes. He can't be there.'

Caines walked back to the gateway and stared up at the house. Tom had rented the fourth flat, and there were six in all. The house had three storeys, which presumably meant two flats per floor. Which also meant that his window would be one of the two on the first floor. Both were dark.

'What do we do?' Calvin asked.

'There's nothing we can do at the moment,' Caines replied. 'Except go home.'

Upstairs, Tom Gibbons was sitting at the grimy window, peering down at Calvin and Caines but taking care to be sure that they couldn't see him. Finally they returned to their respective cars and drove away. He felt a sense of relief intermingled with a feeling of abandonment. Calvin had been persistent in ringing the bell, and the noise had almost driven Tom mad. But he had been determined not to answer it. He couldn't talk to anyone at the moment; he just wanted to be alone with his thoughts.

Leaving the window, he sat down on the bed. The place was cramped and grubby, but it was a haven for the moment. On the bedside cabinet was a carton of fried rice and sweet-and-sour pork, both only half eaten. Beside them stood a bottle of gin, unopened. He had thought that he might need the solace of alcohol but had finally decided against it. He had lost almost everything, but he was determined to hang on to his dignity and self-respect.

When Caines arrived at the cottage, he found Alyson in the throes of packing for the trip to Wembley. In the paddock stood the brand-new horsebox which he had hired and had delivered to the cottage that afternoon.

'What do you think of it?' he asked her.

'It's wonderful!' But she looked worried. 'You didn't buy it, did you?'

'Don't worry, it's rented. I thought you and Thomas should travel in style.'

She flung her arms around him and planted a kiss on his cheek.

'Harry, I can't thank you enough. For everything.'

Caines surprised himself by blushing.

'That will do nicely,' he said.

# *Chapter Seventeen*

Bacon and eggs were sizzling merrily in the frying pan when Annie entered from the bedroom. It was a warm morning, and she was wearing only a plain nightshirt, unbuttoned to the midriff.

Calvin grinned at her approvingly.

'Now that's what I call a beautiful sunrise,' he said.

She smiled and pecked him on the cheek. They had made love well into the night, and with a passion even greater than ever. There had been something almost desperate about it, Calvin thought, as though it was their last night together. Annie had insisted that she *would* be coming back from her trip, but Calvin still felt uneasy and his cheerfulness was somewhat forced.

He dished out the breakfast and they both ate hungrily. Annie's hair was tousled and her lips were full from all the kissing they had done. She looked simply adorable.

They sipped their coffees in silence while birds twittered and chirped in the garden outside. Calvin felt subdued again, at a loss.

'You'd better be getting ready,' he said presently. 'Otherwise you'll miss the morning tide.'

'There is time,' she told him. 'I will bring you a present from Dartmouth. And you will bring me a present from Wembley?'

He had told her that he was going to watch Alyson in the Foxhunter, and she had approved. He nodded. 'What would you like?'

'A lucky horseshoe, perhaps? And a promise not to flirt with any of those beautiful lady showjumpers.'

'I wouldn't dream of it.'

And for the first time in Calvin's adult life, this was true. He had always had a roving eye, no matter how enamoured he was of his current girlfriend; but since Annie had come into his life, he hadn't looked at anyone else.

'Well,' she said, 'perhaps I will go and get dressed.'

She disappeared into the bedroom, and emerged ten minutes later wearing a chunky dark blue sweater, jeans and sturdy boots. The complete seawoman.

'I'll come down to the yacht with you,' Calvin said.

She shook her head. 'It is only Dartmouth, Calvin. I am not sailing to America.'

She came forward and kissed him on the lips.

'Any idea what time you'll be back?' he asked.

'There is a moon tonight, and I will sail under it. By night, the sea is beautiful, no? So I do not rush. I will find a warm bed with a warm sleeping Calvin inside it when I return, *ja*?'

Finally she departed. Through the kitchen window, Calvin watched her walk down the path towards the river. Her yacht was hidden behind a stand of willows, and she waved at him before she disappeared behind them. He wanted to run after her.

He had a few hours to kill before he was due to leave to pick up Bruce and Nigel for the drive to London. He moped about the cottage, washing up, tidying, thinking of Annie all the time. Eventually he walked down to the riverbank. But she was long gone and would doubtless be out at sea by now, as free as a bird.

Calvin returned to the cottage and busied himself with other household chores. He checked the Renault over to make sure that it was ready for the drive to London. Everything was in order.

There was still half an hour before he was due to leave. He took a long shower, and afterwards dressed in a blazer and roll-necked sweater. Finally it was time to leave.

Nigel and Bruce were waiting for him outside the Custom

House in Wrelling. Bruce was soberly attired in a herringbone suit and tie, whereas Nigel wore a rather garish Norfolk jacket with an even more garish paisley cravat at his neck.

'What's this?' Calvin remarked to him. 'You look like Little Lord Fauntleroy.'

'He thinks cravas are *de rigueur* at horse shows,' Bruce said.

Calvin grinned, feeling some of his normal good humour returning. 'Sometimes I wonder about you, Nigel. I really do.'

Wembley. Caines had not imagined that the atmosphere would be so electric. The stadium was filled with over ten thousand people, and the air of excitement and anticipation was almost palpable.

Caines stood in the competitors' enclosure, staring out. The fences on the course were taller than he had expected, and some of them looked fearsome – a wall with rails behind, a reversed oxer, the water jump. Alyson had led Thomas around the course earlier and had met several of the other riders – some of them well-known faces. Caines had stayed in the background, watching and listening. He was enjoying himself, though he also felt nervous. Nervous for Alyson and for Thomas. But Alyson herself was flushed with excitement, too thrilled by the occasion to show any anxiety.

She was saddled up, awaiting her call, resplendent in her jacket, breeches and riding hat. And Thomas himself was well-groomed – she had made sure that he followed her instructions to the letter on that.

'Ho!' said a familiar voice.

Calvin, Bruce and Nigel entered. All smiles, they came over. Alyson was concentrating on preparing herself mentally for her first round, but she broke off to exchange a few words with them.

'You look a picture, Aly,' said Nigel.

'So do you,' she replied.

'He forgot the gaiters and the trilby,' Calvin said. 'Let 'em have it, Aly!'

'How are you feeling?' Bruce asked.

'I'm as ready as I'll ever be,' she told him.

At this point the rider out on the course completed his last jump.

'I'm next,' Alyson said, her voice dropping to a whisper as she realized that her time had finally come.

'Good luck!' Caines and the others said in unison.

Then her name was called. She spurred Thomas forward, out into the arena.

A gibbous moon hung over the ocean, backdropping the dark outline of the freighter. Annie stood silently on the deck of her yacht as two crewmen from the ship took the last of her cargo below. Nothing had been left to chance. Charles had supplied her with all the maps she needed, and she had made rendezvous with the freighter out at sea on the stroke of ten P.M.

The smell of cannabis was heavy in the air. It was packed in hand-sized bales, wrapped in tinfoil, brown paper, then an outer covering of polythene. Each bale looked innocuous, yet the cargo was worth hundreds of thousands of pounds. She felt a thrill at the illicitness of it all. She had always been attracted by both wealth and danger, and in Charles Thieron she had found the perfect combination of the two.

The final bale was stacked below. Without a word, the two crewmen climbed back into the boat and began rowing off towards the freighter. Professionals, she thought, not wasting time on frivolous chatter. Businesslike, doing what was necessary without fuss.

She went below to the radio. Charles was waiting for her at the other end of the line.

'All is well,' she told him. 'I am heading in.'

'Do we have what we need?' he asked.

'It is all here.'

'Good. I shall be waiting for you.'

'You were terrific, Aly,' Nigel said.

'Seventh!' she said, beaming. 'I can hardly believe it! I didn't even think I'd make the jump-off.'

'Did you hear the crowd?' remarked Bruce. 'It was like being at a football match.'

'God,' said Calvin, 'those fences looked formidable, Aly. I'd have been terrified.'

'I nearly came a cropper at the parallel bars on the second round,' she told him, 'but Thomas came good at the last moment. He's the real hero.'

They had driven back to Alyson's cottage after the event, and Caines had just uncorked a magnum of champagne in celebration.

'To Thomas!' said Nigel, raising his glass.

'To Thomas!' echoed the others, and they toasted the horse.

The horsebox which Caines had rented stood outside the front window. As Caines swallowed his champagne, he saw Alyson give him a quiet smile of gratitude.

'Another toast,' she said. 'To Harry, without whom none of this would have been possible.'

'To Harry,' said the others, obviously enjoying the opportunity to drop all formalities with their boss for once.

Then Alyson looked thoughtful.

'And to Chris,' she said quietly. 'We did it for him.'

They drank a respectful toast. But the mood of solemnity quickly evaporated as the talk turned once more to Alyson's performance. She had wisely opted to get around the course with as few faults as possible and not worry too much about her time. This policy had proved the correct one: apart from the near-disaster at the parallel bars, she had never been in serious danger of being thrown or having Thomas refuse a fence. On the day she had done far better than many more experienced riders.

The celebration went on, and more champagne flowed. But presently Calvin began to look restless.

'Well,' he said, 'I'd better be getting back.'

Nigel glanced at his watch. 'It's still early.'

'Things to do.'

Bruce eyed him. 'Not like you to leave a party before it's finished, Cal.'

Calvin tried to make light of it. 'Must be getting old. I'll see you all tomorrow.'

At the door he gave Alyson a big kiss. 'Well done again, Aly. After all you've been through, this is a real triumph. I'm delighted for you.'

Then he left, walking through the gathering dark to his car. He had enjoyed celebrating Alyson's success, but he hadn't been entirely able to stop thinking about Annie. He wanted to get home, to be there when she returned.

Lovesick, he thought to himself as he started up the car. You're behaving like a lovesick kid. But there was nothing he could do about it.

He drove home, taking the route which would lead him on to the road which ran parallel to the towpath. But there was no sign of Annie's yacht on the riverbank as he approached the cottage. It was not yet midnight, and she had told him she would be late.

He made himself a mug of drinking chocolate and sat down in an armchair. Five minutes later, the telephone rang.

Convinced that it was Annie, he snatched it up.

He heard the pips of a public telephone, then a coin being slotted in.

'Cal?' said a voice which he immediately recognized.

'Tom,' he said. 'Where are you?'

'Cal, I know it's late, but I need to talk to someone.'

'Where are you?'

'A call-box on the corner of the street. That was my last ten pence piece.'

'Come on over. I'm here on my own.'

'No car, Cal. Can you come here?'

Calvin had forgotten. He glanced at his Rolex Oyster: it was just after midnight.

'You sound a bit groggy, Tom. Have you been hitting the hard stuff?'

'I haven't slept for the past twenty-four hours. Are you coming over, Cal?'

Calvin was assuming that Annie would return in the next hour or so, and he wanted to be there to greet her. But he hesitated only momentarily. Tom was his friend, and needed his help.

'I'll drive over now,' he began.

But the pips had started, drowning out his words. He waited for the brief silence at the end of them before the cut-off tone in which to tell Tom he was coming. But the line went abruptly dead.

Calvin left immediately, not bothering to lock the front door. He thought of scribbling a note to Annie to let her know where he'd gone, but he didn't want to waste a second. Tom sounded exhausted and desperate.

The midnight streets were silent, empty, and everything looked dark and ominous under the harsh sodium-orange glow of the streetlamps. Calvin drove at speed to Tom's place, praying that he would not do anything foolish. He was unused to thinking gloomy thoughts, but he had felt apprehensive all day, as if disaster was looming.

Turning into Tom's street, he saw the phone-box on the corner. It was empty. But a light was burning in one of the second-floor windows, and the front door was open.

Calvin climbed the stairs and knocked on the door of the fourth flat.

'It's open.'

Tom was lying on his bed, his hands behind his head. Calvin had anticipated that he would look haggard and distraught, but he did not. A day's stubble covered his chin and his eyes were puffy with sleeplessness, but otherwise he seemed all right.

'I didn't think you were coming,' he said.

'You know me better than that, Tom. I tried to tell you I was on my way, but the blasted pips started.'

'I didn't get my ten penceworth, that's for sure.'

'Are you all right?'

'I feel like hell, but that's mainly lack of sleep. I was tossing and turning most of the night, running things over in my mind. I was also here last night when you called. Didn't feel like talking then, so I didn't answer the bell.'

'I understand.'

'Do you? Then perhaps you can explain it to me.'

'Explain what?'

'How I got into this mess.'

Calvin sat down on the corner of the bed. 'God knows, Tom, I'm the last person you should ask that question of. You know me – jump in first, think later. I'm not the analytical type.'

'No,' Tom agreed. Then he looked thoughtful. 'Remember the old days? Both of us bachelor gays –'

'Hey, steady on. "Gay" has got a different meaning these days.'

'– playing the field, free and easy as birds. Now you're in love and I'm all washed up.'

'Washed up? That's a bit strong. Caines would probably –'

'I don't want to talk about Caines. Or the job. Or even Sue. My big mistake was not seeing earlier what a spoiled, selfish bitch she was.'

Calvin said nothing.

'I take your silence for agreement, Cal. If it wasn't for the kids, I'd be glad it's over.'

'Maybe you need a holiday.'

It sounded trite as soon as it was out, but Tom did not take offence.

'Maybe I do. And maybe that's what I am doing. Taking a break from everyone.' He gave a deep sigh. 'I don't really know why I asked you to come here, Cal. I think I just wanted someone to listen, not offer any solutions. I know I have to sort things out for myself in the end.'

'But friends can help. You know we'll do what we can. You can call on me whenever you need to.'

'I appreciate that, Cal. I really do.'

There was silence for a moment. Then Tom said, 'Want a drink?'

Calvin saw the bottle of gin on the bedside cabinet. It had not been opened.

'Not for me,' he said. 'I had a few glasses of champagne earlier, celebrating Alyson's success in the Foxhunter.'

'I forgot. How did she do?'

'She came seventh.'

'Good for her. Makes you think – she's had it far rougher than me, but she's coping.'

'She relied on her friends, Tom. Caines has been a big help to her.'

'Caines, yes. I'm still not sure what to make of the man.'

'He took you in when you needed a place.'

'Then tried to get me transferred when the going got rough.'

'It was just a recommendation, Tom. I think he had your best interests in mind. When he asked me what I thought of the idea, I had to agree with him. You couldn't go on as you've been doing.'

'So you've come round to his way of thinking, have you?'

'I think he's proved that he's straight. Tough, but straight. At least you know where you are with the man. You could ask for worse Surveyors.'

'Like me, for example.'

'I didn't mean that.'

'No, that was unfair.'

Again there was silence. Tom stared out the dark window.

'How's Annie?' he asked.

'She's all right,' Calvin said.

'You don't sound very confident about that.'

'Perhaps I'm not. I have this feeling that things are not going to work out between us. As if I'm skating over thin ice.'

He had been denying the feeling until now, but having spoken of it, it seemed real. He shrugged and attempted his old heartiness: 'Not to worry, old son, eh? They come and they go.'

'They do indeed, Cal. But I hope things work out better for you and Annie than they did for me and Sue.'

They talked on for well over an hour, concentrating on the old days, when things had been much freer and simpler. It seemed to Calvin that Tom was still delaying facing up to his various problems, but he himself was quite happy to dwell on the past for a while since his own immediate future suddenly seemed uncertain.

At length Tom began to look tired, his eyelids drooping.

'I think I'm going to be sleeping soon,' he said. 'You'd better be getting home to that woman of yours.'

'I'll stay if you want me to.'

'No, it's all right. I'll be fine now.'

'Are you sure?'

'Positive. Sleep's what I need. You go home.'

But Calvin lingered for a further half hour until he was sure that Tom was soundly asleep. Then he pulled the coverlet over him and departed, closing the door quietly behind him.

Charles had been waiting for her on the quayside of a secluded cove. The cannabis had been quickly loaded into a transit van, which would already be on its way to London. Now she was heading home.

Her watch showed two-thirty. Calvin would doubtless be fast asleep, and she would take a bath before joining him in bed. There was a china model of a sailor in her cabin which she had bought the previous day in Wrelling High Street for a few pounds. She would tell Calvin that it was an antique which she had picked up in Dartmouth; he would not know the difference. The figure was bearded and cheerful, but with also a suggestion of innocence. Just like her dear, unsuspecting Calvin, in fact.

She moored the yacht at the quayside near the cottage and went ashore. Beyond the willow trees, the cottage was in darkness. She smiled, imagining Calvin snoring gently in his sleep. The moon had set hours ago, but the stars were brilliant in the sky above.

Calvin had left the door on the latch for her. She entered the cottage silently, switching on the table lamp. All was quiet, and the bedroom door was closed.

'Cal?' she said, not too loudly.

There was no reply; he was evidently fast asleep.

She picked up the telephone and began dialling Charles Thieron's number.

Calvin had just got out of the car when he spotted the masts of Annie's yacht near the quayside. She was coming in without lights, and Calvin's suspicions were immediately aroused. He felt a sinking in the pit of his stomach, but at the same time he wasn't entirely surprised. He had been deluding himself in thinking that Annie was playing straight with him, and now the instincts of a Customs officer overtook him.

Without actually hiding, Calvin waited near the line of willows. He watched Annie mooring the yacht. A few minutes later, she came ashore, heading towards the cottage without noticing him. Calvin smelt something in the air. Approaching the yacht, he was greeted with the faint but characteristic odour of cannabis resin.

A swift check of the hold revealed that the cannabis had already been offloaded, but doubtless there would be traces of it from where a bale had been cut open for the courier to check that it was the authentic substance. He hurried up to the cottage, lifting the latch very gently and easing the door open.

Through the crack he saw Annie standing with her back to him in the soft yellow glow of the table-lamp, the telephone in her hand.

'Charles?' she was saying. 'It's Annie. Did the consignment get away safely?'

She listened for a moment, then said, 'Good. Everything is fine here. . . He is asleep, I think. Sleeping the sleep of the just, *ja*?'

She laughed, and Calvin felt more betrayed than ever.

'Goodnight, Charles,' she was saying. 'I will see you soon, and then we will celebrate.'

She put the telephone down and walked into the bathroom. Presently Calvin heard the sound of water running in the bath. He waited five minutes before creeping into the living room and picking up the phone.

The ringing of the phone woke Caines from a deep sleep. He sat up, feeling a little groggy. He had stayed at Alyson's until midnight, finishing off the magnum of champagne with Bruce and Nigel. They had all drunk a little too much, so finally Alyson had phoned for a taxi to ferry them all home.

Caines got out of bed and picked up the phone.

'Mr Caines?' said a whispered voice.

'Yes?'

'It's Calvin, sir. I'm at my cottage. I think you ought to come over here right away.'

'What the devil is going on, Calvin? Why are you

whispering?'

'I've got a viper in the nest, sir. She needs her fangs pulled.'

Calvin sat in the armchair beside the fireplace, waiting for Annie to emerge from the bathroom and for Caines to arrive. He understood now why she had not wanted him to wait up for her. She had probably guessed that the yacht would carry the tell-tale smells of cannabis for a few hours after she had offloaded the cargo and had not wanted him sniffing around.

His humiliation was made more intense by his conviction that the 'Charles' she had been addressing on the phone was none other than his old enemy, Thieron. He had no evidence of that at the moment, of course, but it all made perfect sense. He remembered how she had sidetracked him at the marina when Thieron had come ashore with the birdbox, and now it seemed deliberate. Annie had probably come to England for the express purpose of acting as a courier for a drugs shipment. And Thieron was at the centre of it all, he was sure. No doubt the cannabis would be on its way to London by now. And if Tom hadn't phoned him up, he would still be fast asleep and none the wiser of Annie's treachery.

You were stupid, Calvin, he told himself, a lovesick idiot. But his anger was coloured with a deep hurt. He had always been a romantic type, but with Annie he had begun to think that he had actually discovered true love for the first time. But all the while she had been playing him for a sucker.

He had told Caines the whole story over the phone, talking quietly so that Annie would not hear him from the bathroom. Caines was coming over by taxi, and he would stop off first at the yacht to confirm the smell of cannabis before it faded away. Then Annie would be taken in for questioning.

Calvin rose and went over to the window. It was still dark outside. What a day it had been: Alyson's triumph and his humiliation. But he'd survive; he'd bounce back.

He saw the taxi pull up near the towpath. Caines got out and walked down towards the yacht. Behind him, the bathroom door opened.

Annie appeared, a white towel wrapped around her midriff.

'Calvin,' she said with surprise. 'You're up.'

'Indeed I am.'

'I thought you were asleep.'

'Oh, no. I've been out for a drive. And a little walk.'

He saw a hint of nervousness before she disguised it with one of her flashing smiles.

'Have a nice trip?' he asked.

She shook her head. 'It was most unsatisfactory. I found nothing I wanted, except there is something I get for you.'

She indicated an object on the coffee table which was wrapped in white tissue paper.

'What is it?' he asked.

'Take the paper off and see.'

He did not move from the window. 'I forgot your horseshoe.' He was surprised that it had, in fact, slipped his mind.

She moved towards him. 'Is something wrong, Cal? I am sorry it is so late. I was coming to join you in bed, fresh from the bath.'

Her beauty still moved him deeply, but he resisted her blue eyes and the provocative tone of her voice.

'I saw you come in, Annie. Without lights. I smelled the cargo you've been carrying. Then I came back here and heard you on the telephone. Who's Charles? Is it Thieron?'

Suddenly there was a hard glint in her blue eyes. She said nothing. He saw Caines coming up the path to the cottage.

'You'd better get dressed,' he said, only just keeping his voice steady. 'You won't be sleeping in my bed again.'

There was a knocking on the door.

Caines and Calvin stood on the quay of the marina early the following morning, watching Thieron's cruiser pull out. They had spent half the night interviewing Annie, and both men were tired. She had not tried to deny her part in smuggling the cannabis ashore, but she had refused to give them details of the operation and had refused to implicate Thieron. The Frenchman was standing on the prow of the cruiser as it passed them, and he gave a cheery wave.

'Good morning, gentlemen,' he said. 'A beautiful morning, *n'est-ce pas*?'

It's almost as if he knew how close we were to getting him, Caines thought.

Calvin scowled at Thieron as he drifted by.

'Cocky devil,' he muttered. 'I'd like to wring his neck.'

'His time will come, Calvin,' said Caines. 'We just have to be patient.'

Caines felt frustrated but not entirely dissatisfied. After taking Annie Soldstrom in for questioning he had telephoned the Investigation Division in London and had warned them that a consignment of cannabis was en route to London. The tip had paid off: only an hour later he had received a call from Chris Lucas's colleague Adam Bellman to inform him that the consignment had been seized on its delivery to a house which had been under surveillance by ID officers. Again no connection with Thieron had been established, but the seizure of the cannabis would be a big blow to his operations.

Caines stared at the white water in the cruiser's wake. He had another reason for feeling positive about the future. That afternoon he was due to be interviewed by the Assistant Collector, and Charles Christie had already rung him to indicate that the team system which he had initiated at Wrelling was being viewed with approval and would be allowed to continue. It hadn't worked totally smoothly, of course: Tom Gibbons had been a casualty, but through circumstances over which none of them had had any control. But Alyson, Calvin, Bruce, Nigel and the rest of the staff now seemed to have adapted to the new regime and were actually benefiting from it. They were more flexible and efficient. Thieron was still at large, but the first cracks had begun to appear in his criminal organization, and Caines remained hopeful that the whole edifice would soon crumble. A lot would depend on their alertness and diligence in the weeks and months which lay ahead.

'What now, sir?' Calvin asked.

'Now,' said Caines, 'it's time we remembered that chasing smugglers is only a small fraction of our work. It's time that normal business was resumed.'

Calvin looked slightly apprehensive. 'Does that mean paperwork, sir?'

'Yes it does, Calvin – among other things. But no doubt we'll be able to find time for you to take the launch out now and again.'

Calvin grinned and stared out at the grey-blue waters of the harbour, his thoughts of Annie already less painful.

'Ahh,' he said. 'That's music to my ears, sir.'